During the co
Robertson has been an author,
journalist, advertising agent, pig farmer and dairy farmer. He lives with his family in Somerset and is in great demand as an after-dinner speaker.

Also by James Robertson:

Any Fool Can Be a Pig Farmer
Any Fool Can Be a Dairy Farmer
Any Fool Can Be a Countryman
Any Fool Can Be a Villager
Any Fool Can Be a Country Lover
Any Fool Can Keep a Secret

The Devon Book
The Somerset Book
The Cornwall Book
The Avon Book

Any Fool Can Be a Yokel

James Robertson

Illustrated by Larry

HEADLINE

First published in Great Britain in 1985
by Pelham Books Ltd

First published in paperback in Great Britain in 1988
by HEADLINE BOOK PUBLISHING PLC

ISBN 0 7472 3128 1

Printed and bound in Great Britain by
Collins, Glasgow

HEADLINE BOOK PUBLISHING PLC
Headline House
79 Great Titchfield Street
London W1P 7FN

Chapter One

THE CLOCK in the church tower had stopped. It was a church clock with all the necessary trimmings. It had its moping owl; it overlooked the graveyard where the rude forefathers of the hamlet heaved the turf in mouldering heaps. Its tower had even been ivy-mantled until a decade earlier when it had been decided that Virginia creeper would be less damaging to the stonework. It was more appropriate anyway, since the building was dedicated to the beautiful St Wilgefort who had grown a beard to discourage suitors and retain her virginity. But the clock had worked for a good couple of centuries, tolling out the days and seasons for the good folk of the village who lay or got laid in its shadow.

They had grown to depend on it. Its mellow chime was less obvious than it had been in the past as it was often drowned by the noise of traffic or the slurping of ice-cream-eating tourists who wandered the streets of the village, gawping at the thatched cottages and leaning over the medieval bridge to look at the trout which disported themselves in the river below. But its chime was still important. During the still watches of the night, it rang down the wooded valley and bounced off the steep hillsides. Then the clock's habit of losing eight minutes a day came into its own, persuading shy virgins, admittedly as rare as unicorns in the parish, that it was not time to return to their cottages and farmsteads quite yet, and allowing the pub to stay open for a few more precious minutes which, by the day before it was wound, would have stretched to a useful three-quarters of an hour.

The clock had stopped a couple of times before. The most

serious occasion had been during the war when the sexton had suffered a severe attack of delirium tremens brought on by a surfeit of scrumpy. He had been convinced that the Germans were about to invade and had barricaded himself in the church tower armed with tins of stewed plums and an air-gun with which he proposed to shoot birds which he would then tie to the lightning conductors to be flash-fried during thunder-

storms for his meals. He had chosen the glorious Spitfire summer of 1940. While the Few carved their legend in the skies over Kent, the cloudless heaven above the village was tainted by the subtle odour emanating from a hundred rotting sparrows. This was eventually overlaid by the awesome bouquet of the excrement resulting from an exclusive diet of stewed plums which rained down on the ground from the top of the tower.

On that occasion the clock had just not been wound. This time it was broken. The commander, who ran a market garden at the bottom of the village, had wanted to try his hand at bell ringing. He had become bored by grandsires and treble bobs after a couple of hours and most of a bottle of gin, and had attempted to play the sailor's hornpipe, but he had swung from the clock weight instead of a bell rope by mistake. When the verger had next climbed the spiral staircase to the top of the tower to spend his usual sweaty fifteen minutes amid the cobwebs and bat droppings in turning the handle that brought the weights up from the floor, they refused to come. Something was bent.

The verger reported the matter to the pub. This was the hub of village life where most of the influential figures of the neighbourhood gathered once – if not twice – a day in the public bar to consult with each other on matters of local concern. The pub despatched Frank Mattock to repair the clock. Frank was a farmer, now in his forties, who had risen from being an assistant slaughterman to owner-occupying dairy farmer through an astonishing run of good fortune which began with the premium bonds, progressed through the pools and had had its most recent manifestation in a disgustingly large sum of money won from the *Reader's Digest* in one of those free contests that every sensible person throws in the rubbish bin as soon as they come through the letterbox. Frank had a tendency to put on weight, a fact that was always evident as he also liked to go around in white shirts unbuttoned to the navel which showed off his hairy, tubular torso and the chunky jewellery that usually bounced away on top of it. Frank, like all farmers, could mend anything. Give a farmer a hammer and a piece of baler twine and he would confidently approach the faulty guidance equipment on a space shuttle.

Frank hit the clock mechanism once or twice and slid his crowbar into the works, levering it a few times so that some bits dropped off and shattered on the church floor 50 feet below. He then reported his failure back at the pub. An expert quoted £500, which was a large sum of money, to repair the damage. The commander was not going to pay: he had only bent something; and Frank said that *he* could not be held responsible for metal fatigue – one bit had shattered after only a single hammer blow. The vicar, a dangerous radical who had once proposed sending the proceeds of the Sunday collection to the families of striking miners, was approached but he thought that the clock might as well stay broken since everybody who wanted to know the time had a watch already. The village was faced with the need to find £500.

One would not have thought that the raising of such a sum would have presented many difficulties. The average English village conceals an astonishing amount of money. Take the land alone. The parish had a couple of thousand acres of farmland, most of which was owned by a dozen or so individuals who could be seen nightly in the pub, nursing half-pints in their gnarled hands and wearing gumboots and trousers held up with baler twine: there was £4 million or so there. Then there was the village itself. To the irritation of most of those who had been born there, it was beautiful. The river which ran through it chuckled and sparkled. Many of the streets were cobbled, winding, narrow and given an added dimension by the millstreams which popped up here and there for a few yards before plunging back beneath the ground through neatly arched stone tunnels. Most of the cottages were thatched and lime-washed pink, green or white and looked as if any one of them could easily have housed Red Riding Hood's grandmamma or a gargantuan Squirrel Nutkin. The entire picture-postcard conglomeration was set at the top of a steep-sided valley whose thickly wooded slopes made an eminently satisfactory backcloth for all the amateur photographers who snapped the same things from the same angles every year.

If only, bemoaned the locals, the village was ugly. Dot a few slag heaps around; knock down the string of seventeenth-century cottages that lined the banks of the river and ask a fashionable architect to fill the space with modern living modules – anything that would drive the tourists away and give all the residents a bit of privacy. However, the picturesqueness of the community brought in money. The tourists may have clogged the pavements with their peeling bodies and their cars may have filled the roads like flocks of mechanized sheep, but they were sheep that could be fleeced. Those who did not work on the land worked on the tourists and took money off them through cafes, souvenir shops, garages and bed-and-breakfast establishments. And the prettiness of the place brought in the wealthy retired, drunks every one, who enabled the village grocer to sell expensive guavas, pawpaws and smoked salmon as well as Chateaux Latour, Lafite, d'Yquem and twenty different varieties of malt whisky. The village was rich but did its best to conceal the fact. One could never quite be sure that one of those innocent-seeming tourists might not be a tax inspector.

The pub was discussing some serious business. Nothing mundane like money or politics, but a good titillating local scandal – the staff of life. Bill slowly supped a mouthful of beer from the thin-walled glass that had been standing on the oak bar against which he had been leaning. He replaced the glass and smacked his lips to remove the line of froth that had stuck to them. He turned back to his attentive audience of fellow drinkers, enjoying his recapitulation of the events so far: 'Well, David Carter is having a dalliance with Maureen Reed.'

Everyone knew this already and had done for a week or more, but there was a sucking-in of breath from the others. David Carter, his wife and their three small children lived only a few doors up from the pub. 'He must be near thirty-five and she is only twenty-one,' continued Bill. There was a shaking of heads. 'Mary Mowbray's younger sister is Sharon

Carter – David's wife – and she and Angela Reed, Maureen's mother, have been best friends ever since they left school. But not now they ain't!' Bill paused on that triumphant note. There was complete silence from the others – elderly farmers, gamekeepers, farm workers and a smattering of ex-tourists who had bought property and settled. The only sound was the measured ticking of the clock, the hiss of damp wood from the sullen fire that smoked reluctantly in the inglenook and the faint sounds from the juke box that thumped away all day and night in the tourist ghetto of the lounge bar through the thick cob wall.

'Granny Reed and Granny Carter have fallen out too. And they're sisters and have always said they'd never had a cross word between them since they were two!'

Kelvin pursed his lips sanctimoniously. He, like Bill, was an elderly farmer. Bill had retired, in theory, which meant that he lived off deals and land rents. In fact he did very well at it and was rumoured to keep great wads of notes inside the dirty trilby hat that never left his head. Kelvin still actively farmed which meant, in his case, that he told his daughter what to do each morning before going off to market or out on some other errand. 'It's a right bad business,' he said.

Bill had not finished yet. 'And yesterday morning, right in the street, Stephanie Jarrett saw George Carter strike his son and call him a stupid bastard.' A mass clicking of tongues ensued.

'I hear that Maureen is having to move out of the village to let things cool down a bit,' said Keith. He was a butcher in his fifties who had caused a great stir when he had moved to the village a couple of years earlier and, with his wife, had prettified a perfectly innocuous cottage so that it looked like the sort of place that Hansel and Gretel might inhabit in a Disney cartoon.

It was a wonderful scandal and it had to be spelled out in every salacious detail at each social gathering, after which all its ramifications and possible scenarios would be examined. Once the essential facts had been set out, the imaginations of everyone could roam free and flesh them out where they felt like.

The village enjoyed a *brouhaha* of these dimensions every decade or so and had done for several centuries. They were colossal while they lasted, a source of deep pleasure and satisfaction to everyone in the village who was not directly involved. But the place was small; people had to continue to live together and scandals always blew over with, perhaps, a shuffle of the pack of human cards before they settled down again. The very smallness of the village always prevented too much calumny being cast at the sinners. If one became too self-righteous, there was the risk that some dark secret from one's own past or that of one's father or grandfather might be recalled as a reproof to one's hypocrisy. It was amazing how many 'sisters' existed who were in reality daughters, the result of harvest indiscretions during giddy girlhood. There was even an entire generation, born during the war, whose paternity owed considerably more to the convalescent home for battle-fatigued American soldiers than to the regular swains of the village who could not compete either financially or charismatically with those exotic foreigners who spoke like they did in the films that were sometimes shown on Saturday night in the church hall.

This latest scandal was lumbering along its predictable path. Maureen would have to leave the area for a year or two before returning to marry and settle down to produce children and prepare packed lunches for whichever farm worker would end up as her husband. The pub customers puffed at their pipes in companionable silence as they remembered their youth when they too had possessed the capacity to become the central figure in such a scandal.

'Sex,' said Bill suddenly. The others cocked a pensive eye at him. 'If this village has got to get some money to pay for this here clock, something to do with sex is the best way to raise it. Everybody is interested in sex. The young want to know all about it. Most people want to know how to do more of it and those like us want to remember how it was.'

'That's true,' agreed Kelvin. 'There's money in sex. Look at Nellie.' Everybody thought about Nellie. Thirty years ago, when anyone complained that the village was staid or dull,

Nellie would be pointed out. She lived in a cottage equidistant from three villages and cycled round the countryside serving her exclusive clientele. Nellie and her bicycle were available for hire; she was the district's sole representative of the demimonde. Even in those days, Nellie had struggled to make a good enough living for herself and the four children which were the byproducts of her chosen profession; there were too many enthusiastic amateurs around. But her customers had grown old with her and had remained loyal. She had given up riding her bike and could often be seen striding along the road to the village in her woolly balaclava with wispy grey hair poking out from underneath, a ridiculously unglamorous figure with her bright little face highlighted by large round spectacles through which she peered shortsightedly at the world around her. Nowadays her clients visited her in their battered motor cars and on their tractors, but the local convention was that nobody knew about it. Nellie was treated as a colourful figure from the past and was cherished as the only practising hooker in six parishes.

'You could hardly say that Nellie has grown rich on sex,' objected Jimmy. He was the oldest man in the village and, as such, occupied the Windsor chair that sat by the fireplace. He was a tiny, bandy-legged old man who would have been far more comfortable on the stool he had been used to all his drinking life, but he had enough of a sense of history and duty to do what was expected of him.

'She's done all right,' replied Bill, idly rolling himself a cigarette with one hand, a widespread skill learned on tractors. 'We only want £500 for the clock and she must bring in a damn sight more than that each year. So there's willingness to spend money on sex round about.'

'True enough,' admitted Jimmy. 'But her money comes from people like Kelvin and there aren't many like him.'

Kelvin began to splutter with outrage. The fact that he was one of Nellie's friends could hardly be a secret since the battered, doorless ex-post office van that he drove around was there to be seen parked outside her door on alternate Wednesday nights and it could even be heard as it blared through the village with its defective exhaust on the way there. There was not much he could say in denial and Bill saved him the trouble of trying.

'We've got to tap into the female market. The women folk don't spend nearly enough money on sex.'

'Ah, but if they did, it would be our money,' replied Jimmy, which was a bit of a cheek on his part since he and most of those present were either bachelors or widowers.

At this point the door of the pub opened and Lindy walked in. One of the curious aspects of village mores was that women were always treated as gross inferiors and drudges only so long as they allowed themselves so to be. The ordinary housewife was scarcely of more import than a milch-cow until she decided to nag or assert herself, whereupon her husband would crumble and the other men of the village would regard her as a terrible force of nature. If a woman took a job or became prominent outside the home, she was treated as an equal or superior by the most chauvinistic or arrogant of the locals. It was as if she lost her gender. Women, in the eyes of the average local male, was the word given to those females who stayed at home to smooth the lives of the superior sex. Once they broke out of that mould, they became something different. The usual courtesies due to their sex were dropped and they were expected to exchange opinions and blue jokes with anyone.

Lindy was the epitome of this latter stage of womanhood. She was married and had two small children but she brought in the bulk of her family's income through her job as district nurse. At the end of her day, she liked to come into the pub for a quick lager while her husband cooked the dinner. She was a short woman in her thirties, highly efficient at her job and had the dedication to walk through the winter snowdrifts in order to change a dressing or to comfort one of her elderly patients. She was built rather on the lines of Dolly Parton, but the locals would no more dream of lusting after her than they would after the parson.

'What are you lot talking about?' was her greeting.

'Sex,' replied Bill succinctly.

'Ah! You mean the David Carter business.'

'No, we weren't talking about that,' replied Bill.

Lindy gave him a sceptical glance. 'You must have been the only people in the village who weren't. Gossip keeps this place going.'

'It's not gossip,' replied the commander loftily. 'It's the study of human nature which is the foundation of all art and culture.'

Lindy let that one go. 'In that case, what about sex?'

'We were thinking about ways to raise the money for the clock bill and sex seemed to be one of the few interests shared by everybody that we could think of that might be exploitable.'

'I don't see how you can make much money out of sex round here,' objected Lindy. 'Nellie has got the market sewn up. Ask Kelvin.'

Kelvin began to splutter again. 'I strongly object to remarks and insinuations like that being made about me.'

'I don't see that you've got much to complain about since they're true,' replied Bill brutally. 'No, what we reckon,

Lindy, is that we ought to get the women involved. People like Kelvin pay money and Maud at the post office sells lots of dirty magazines each month, but they're all for the men. The women don't spend on anything like that.'

'We're too sensible as a sex. Don't you agree, Helga?'

Helga had just come through from the lounge. She was the current landlord who had taken over the pub just under a year ago and was very different from the usual run of country women. She was an Austrian in her mid-forties and still startlingly beautiful. She was blonde with high cheek bones and wide-set blue eyes and exuded sexuality with the prolific ease of a fountain gushing forth water. She was not a dumb blonde but carried herself with an air of sophisticated central European decadence. She evoked Bond-filled casinos, luxury express trains and black satin sheets. She had earned her living as an actress and, from the few hints that she dropped, she seemed also to have been one of the very last great *poules de luxe*, which was probably how she came to afford to buy the pub.

Initially, the locals had found Helga extremely hard to cope with. If one were male, a conversation with her at a party was an overwhelming experience as she was extremely tactile. For the first two minutes as she greeted you, her hands would be everywhere, stroking and patting and seemed to rummage into every orifice of your body. You felt as if you were being assaulted by a swarm of butterflies. Even as simple an act as offering her a smoke would take on immense sexual significance as she caressed the proffered cigarette first between her fingers and then rolled it sensually between her lips before taking the hand which offered a light between her own and sliding her fingers round the shape of your knuckles and up to the wrist. It left the local men with steam coming out of their ears and the women with daggers from their eyes.

Then it was realized that Helga was no threat. This was her natural way of behaving and she was scrupulous at never doing more than flirt with anyone who was married. If one of the wives of the village saw her husband in a spider-like clinch with Helga in a corner at a party, she did not mind. It was of less significance to Helga than shaking hands and she left the husband in the sort of condition that promised an interesting evening once the wife had got him back home. Helga considered Lindy's point. 'I agree. It is men who make such a fuss about sex. Women do it while men just talk about it.'

When Helga came out with a remark like that, one did not argue, any more than one would with Einstein on the subject of relativity. People were also mesmerized by her voice which was exaggerated Garbo. Like everything else about Helga, it first appeared that she put on this seductive tone and accent by design, but it was entirely natural. It was even a handicap as it had considerably reduced the range of acting parts that she had been considered for in this country. By the time she retired a couple of years before she came to the village, she had become restricted to 'beautiful foreign spies' and Bulldog Drummond-type villainesses.

'What is it that you want to know about sex, anyway, Willie?' Nobody but Helga called Bill by that name. It came out as 'Weelee'.

Bill blushed. Most men blushed when Helga addressed them. It was an embarrassed reflex caused by the carnal thoughts that she invariably aroused. 'I was thinking that a good way to raise money to pay for the clock would be to get some money from the ladies. The Rotary Club made a fortune when they got hold of a stripper in town. Perhaps we could get in a male stripper.'

'A stripper? That would be wonderful, particularly if it was you, my dear.' Bill blushed even deeper. Much of Helga's charm came from the fact that she did not take the way she looked seriously and made fun of the effect that it had on other people. If a remark like that had been made by anyone else, Bill would have been mercilessly mocked, but his cronies held their peace for fear of attracting a machismo-destroying remark from Helga.

'I wouldn't pay money to see a stripper,' said Lindy.

'No. Most men are so disappointing when you see them without their clothes on. It is so much better to leave them with their pride and their cod-pieces intact.'

'I don't wear a cod-piece,' said Kelvin, always slow to learn.

'That is very clear to see, darling.' It came out as 'dorlink'. 'However, I see no reason why we ladies should not have a knicker party.'

The men looked uneasily at each other. 'What *is* a knicker party?' queried the commander.

'You know what a Tupperware party is?' asked Helga. The commander nodded. 'It is the same as that. Except they do not sell plastic containers but all sorts of wonderful things.'

'Like what?' questioned Kelvin.

'You know, beautiful underclothes, vibrators. Things which will make us and our menfolk better lovers. All that sort of stuff. Some of it can be very enjoyable, you know.'

Bill didn't know. It was doubtful if any of those born in the parish would. The commander might know a little about that sort of thing since he had been in the navy and presumably had had a wife in every port. Sex, locally, was a function carried out in the dark in pyjamas on alternate Saturday nights. There was a lot of it about but, after the first careless passions of youth when some experimentation might have been in order, no missionary would be shocked by what he might see. He might, however, be unsettled if he knew the identity of the coupling couples.

There was a pause in the conversation after Helga had revealed a hint of the delights that might be on offer at a knicker party. The locals were rather shaken but they were not going to reveal that to Helga or to each other. Kelvin was the first to put into words some of the *angst* that the others were feeling.

'It won't give our womenfolk any funny ideas, will it?' he asked anxiously. If Nellie had never demonstrated any funny ideas to him, despite her long and varied career, then such things must be few and far between within the locality.

'Oh, Kelvin, don't be so fuddy-duddy. Making love should be fun. Don't you agree?' said Helga. Kelvin had never made love; he had only copulated, so was hardly the right person to ask. 'What about a knicker party, then?' demanded Helga. 'If you want to raise some money, I am sure that I could organize something for the ladies of the village that they would enjoy.'

The establishment of the village began to shuffle their feet and blow through their lips. Bill put their doubts into words.

'I'm not sure that the gentle sex round here are quite ready for that sort of thing. They're not like they are in the city, you know. We menfolk want to protect them from the decline in moral standards.'

'Don't pay any attention to him, Helga. You go right ahead with it,' said Lindy. 'I know the women round here a damn sight better than Bill and this lot, and they would love it.'

'Now look here, Lindy,' protested Bill. 'Don't you go putting any daft ideas into Helga's pretty little head.'

'Oh, Willie. You are so sweet. You are jealous. You would

like to come along to the party yourself. Don't worry, I'll make sure I give you a private showing all of your own and I won't let on to anyone what you buy.'

The solidarity of the opposition began to crumble. 'Here,' said Kelvin, 'if you're going to give Bill a look, I'd like to come along too. And I'm sure most of us would like to as well.'

'In that case, let us have a knicker party for everybody,' said Helga, flinging her arms up in the air. 'I think it would probably be better if we split the sexes though.'

'I don't see why,' objected Kelvin. 'The ladies might like it if their menfolk were beside them to protect them from being embarrassed.'

'It's not the ladies being embarrassed that I'm worried about. It's the men,' replied Helga.

'Don't be daft,' said Kelvin scornfully.

'Helga's right, you know,' said Lindy. 'I think many men would be a bit uneasy to hear women talking openly about sexual matters.'

'Nonsense!' insisted Kelvin stoutly. 'Anyway, the ladies round here just wouldn't talk about things like that.'

'I know at least half a dozen women not very far from this bar who think that their men leave a lot to be desired as lovers.'

The bar was fairly full with several separate groups talking quietly amongst themselves, but all conversation throughout the room ceased immediately. The men pricked up their ears to hear what Lindy would say next and none dared catch the eye of another.

After a short pause, Kelvin cleared his throat nervously: 'Well, I'm all right. I ain't got a woman. Anyway, when would you talk about things like that?'

'You may not have a woman to yourself, Kelvin. But Nellie's a good friend of mine,' said Lindy. The commander gave a guffaw. 'As is your Elfrieda, Commander.' The commander looked thoughtfully into his beer. 'And, you know, we don't just talk about flower arranging at WI meetings. It's astonishing what comes up.'

'Or doesn't come up when it should do,' added Helga.

Bill pulled his handkerchief out of his pocket and trumpeted loudly into the silence. 'Grenville's got a good crop of kale along the top road this year,' he said.

Kelvin eagerly swivelled on his bar stool to look at him.

'I've seen that. I reckon he's hoping to hold a few of the squire's pheasants in there this season.'

Helga and Lindy exchanged a smile which everyone pretended they had not seen as conversations hesitantly re-started.

And so it came to pass that a date was set for the party. It had been hoped to hold it in the church hall, which was the normal venue for events of such importance, but the vicar had expressed grave uncertainty about the bishop's views on such a use for an adjunct of God's house, even though Helga explained to him that frilly knickers were nowhere condemned in the scriptures, not even by St Paul.

The party was then snapped up by Ivor. There was a large chunk of Ivor that had never grown up. While he was a farmer, a sometime county councillor and a member of the board of visitors at the county prison, he still found time to be the prime customer for the rack of dirty video films that had recently been introduced as a sideline in a little room behind the counter of the post office. He had bought most of the magazines which were also on sale there and the range of goods had been extended with the express purpose of retaining his custom. Ivor also took an exhaustingly gleeful delight in dirty jokes. It is traditionally supposed that these find their way, almost by osmosis, into the collective consciousness of all the dirty-joke-telling segments of the world's population at the same time. But Ivor proved it otherwise. Not only did he tell dirty jokes; he invented them as well. Kelvin once said that he had heard one of Ivor's jokes, a subtle play on the bishop-and-actress theme which also involved a fork-lift truck and a monocle, from someone at the market, but most of them were so filthy as to be incomprehensible to everyone else except the squire, though he was so imbued with the concept of *noblesse oblige* that he laughed at everyone's jokes whether he understood them or not.

Ivor had intended to hold the party in his sitting room, but word had gone round very quickly about the sort of entertainment that was going to be on offer, and it was decided to move the venue from his farmhouse to the manor where there would be more room. The squire considered that this might threaten his dignity but Ivor said he would resign his chairmanship of the local Conservative Association if the squire refused, which would mean the latter taking over and, faced with such a threat, he had caved in immediately.

The drawing room of the manor provided an august setting for the party. The grand furniture had been sold off several generations earlier and the collection of paintings had declined to a couple of likenesses of sour-mouthed ancestors that those in the process of founding dynasties had refused to buy and claim as their own. However, provided one ignored the damp stains on the plaster, the odd broken floorboard and the fact that the chimney smoked abominably, it was still an impressive room, despite a few cracked window panes and holes in the panelling caused by the ravages of deathwatch beetle. It was large enough to house the majority of the local adult population who had come along to see what was on offer.

In spite of the ominous nature of Lindy's comments in the pub, which had spread rapidly and secretly to all the males in the community, most of the men had turned out for their party which was to be held first. In exchange for a £1 note each arriving guest was handed a glass of ill-flavoured red wine by Ivor as he came in through the door. The church clock was an excellent cause. The wine had to be decanted as it had been bought by Mick, who ran the local cafe, at a fire-damage sale when a nearby cash-and-carry had burned down after the wiring had been chewed by rats. As the labels had been severely burned – all that was legible was the word 'English' on a few of them – and most of the corks had become loose when the wine had boiled, it had seemed less trouble all round to remove it completely from the bottles. The quality of the wine was not critical as the guests were normally confronted with beverages distilled from the detritus of the hedgerows, quite often pre-sprayed with herbicide which meant that in excess quantities they made effective lawn weedkillers.

The knicker demonstrator at the men's party was a friend of Helga. She was apparently a professional, a full-time knicker-party demonstrator, who had very kindly agreed to pass over her commission to the clock fund, the only condition being that Helga should collect her from the train and have her to stay for the weekend. She was due at 8 pm, which just allowed time for Ivor to go round with his decanter and replenish the glasses. The first evidence that most people had of her arrival was a great booming bellow which silenced all conversation. 'Men! I am having nothing to do with any men!'

Beneath the air of ribald jollity, there was a vein of deep uncertainty among those present and the contempt that came sizzling from the doorway did nothing to alleviate this. People turned to look. Helga, her friend and Lindy, who was carrying a large suitcase, were standing on the threshold. The demonstrator was not what most people had been expecting or even hoping for. Instead of a *Viva Maria* fantasy in frilly clothes, they were confronted with a gorgon. She was much the same age as Helga, but was as different as a carthorse from an Arab. She was certainly blonde and busty, but she was big: not fat, just tall, her hair drawn back in a tight bun above shoulders that would have not been out of place on an American footballer. She wore a pink dress that could have covered tepees for a whole tribe of Indians.

The squire had put a trestle table at one end of the room and this was the platform from which the party was to be run. Helga and the gorgon pushed their way through the guests and the room became silent as they climbed on to the table, using a couple of chairs as ladders, and turned to face the audience. Helga introduced her friend as Lesley Parker-Brown and the woman-mountain rose to her feet to a hearty round of applause. The trestle table creaked ominously as she shifted her weight, surveying the gathering.

'Pay attention, please,' she started, to a rapt audience. 'This party is going to be fun for you all,' she said grimly. 'I am told that Helga has said we intend to show you knickers. This is true but, in addition, there are many other sexual aids and devices that I shall be demonstrating. Normally, as Helga has said, these demonstrations are just for women and we girls thoroughly enjoy ourselves, but you are men which may create certain difficulties. Accordingly, anyone who misbehaves will have to answer to me and I shall eject them from the room. Forcibly, if necessary.' Her eyes swept across the audience. One could have heard a fly fart in the silence. 'Is that clear?' Nobody responded. 'Is that clear?' she repeated, in a voice that would have quelled King Kong. There was hasty agreement from the assembled guests.

'Excellent. Now, these goods are not for the prudish or faint-hearted, so I would suggest that anyone who feels that such things as dildoes, ticklers and extremely revealing undergarments might be embarrassing or offensive to them should leave now.' One could have now heard that same fly's stomach rumble as people strenuously avoided each other's eyes. A couple of young men in the audience nudged each other and one did a poor job in stifling a snort of laughter. Many looked at them enviously as they had the sexual security of youth and probable virginity at their disposal, but Lesley was not to know this. Her cold grey eyes quartered the audience and picked them out with the efficiency of a pin extracting a snail from its fragrantly garlicked shell. The snort became a curious strangled grunt as it froze on the perpetrator's lips. Lesley cleared her throat: 'Sex can be fun, but it is nothing to snigger about.' The two boys blushed deeply and, in the silence which followed, the fly's belly emitted a deafening rumble. The commander, standing by the door, drowned it out in an aside to Ivor. 'I think I'm going. I see no reason why I should stand here and be treated like a primary school child who has just messed his pants. Do you think I could have my money back?'

'For heaven's sake! Don't be so mean. Go, if that's what you want, but at least leave your £1 in the kitty. Remember it was you that bust the clock in the first place.'

'That's right, Ivor,' muttered Kelvin, sidling up just in case he missed anything. 'You tell him. Remember he's drunk the wine and that's what the money was paying for.'

'Don't be absurd,' retorted the commander. 'I saw that wine before it was decanted. If Mick was not paid to take it away, he was robbed!'

'I thought it was quite nice, meself,' mused Kelvin. He was being more discreet than the other two in speaking with his hand in front of his mouth in case the gorgon should spot him. 'It had a round fruity taste, I thought.'

Ivor and the commander turned to look at Kelvin with astonishment. 'What have you been reading?' asked Ivor.

'One of Prudence's magazines,' replied Kelvin. 'By the way, how can a taste be round?'

'It's when you take a good mouthful and it rolls round beneath your tongue – hence "round",' replied the commander. 'Now, about my £1 . . .'

The three of them had been so engrossed in their conversation that they had failed to observe that the gorgon had stopped speaking and was staring at them in fury. The fly and everybody else had, and had been watching the pink tepee cover begin to quiver as the pressure of its owner rose towards the point of explosion. It came. She opened her mouth and let out a mighty roar and, at the same time, she stamped her foot. The table had been suffering considerable discomfort ever since she had clambered aboard it and it had bravely borne its load for as long as it was able, but now it could hold out no more: it gave a loud groan of distress and collapsed.

It is a well-known fact that if one drops a mouse down a mineshaft, it will walk away from the bottom, whereas if one drops a horse down the same shaft, it will messily explode. The same forces of physics applied when the table gave way. Helga let out a squeak of dismay and subsided gracefully into the arms of the squire who had been standing close by, hoping for a peek up her skirt. It had been a vain endeavour since Helga was wearing trousers. Lesley, on the other hand, came down like a factory chimney with half a ton of dynamite to help it on its way. Jimmy had been standing near for much the same reason as the squire and the descending Lesley brushed him aside like a piece of chaff before hitting the floor with a thud that rattled the teeth of every woodworm in the building and brought a squint-eyed squire from an earlier generation crashing down from his vantage point above the fireplace.

There was a moment or two's silence, as in the aftermath of any great natural disaster, before Lesley's bellow of rage and distress was drowned by the clatter of agricultural hobnail boots on the wooden floor as people rushed forward to assist. The squire managed to fight off those who wished to help with Helga while Lindy gave Lesley a cursory examination, diagnosing a severely sprained ankle, and directed a dozen or so bystanders to grasp her by her appendages and carry her from the room. Ivor helpfully held open the door as they staggered past and Lesley ceased her groaning long enough to shoot him a glance that would have melted his spectacles, had he been wearing them.

While Lesley was being treated somewhere in the bowels of the decaying mansion, there was a hiatus at the centre of events. Into this gap sailed Helga. The squire had her seated in an armchair and was enthusiastically patting her hand since it was the only piece of naked flesh that he could reasonably lay his hands upon, but she fought her way free of his sticky grasp. She took firm hold of the suitcase that held Lesley's stock and slammed the lid shut on the fingers of Kelvin who had just realized the fact of its abandonment. She then stood on the armchair and clapped her hands sharply together. 'Pay attention!' she called, turning heads that had moved hopefully towards the large earthenware jug which held the decanted wine. 'It looks as though Lesley is out of action for the rest of the evening, so we can either cancel the party or else I can have a go at demonstration. What do you all want?'

'Will you model for us?' asked Kelvin optimistically.

'You dirty old bugger!' replied Helga cheerfully, to the distress of a local Methodist lay preacher who must have come to the party in error. Helga was a much jollier – if more ignorant – hostess than the expert. She decided to use the armchair as her pulpit and roped in the squire as her assistant. His function was to hold up the suitcase of goodies while Helga delved inside. As he swayed dangerously backwards under the awkward weight of the case, Helga pulled up the first object to cheers from the guests who were feeling like reprieved prisoners since the departure of Lesley. It was made of pink satin and appeared to be about 3 or 4 inches square. Helga looked at it doubtfully and indicated to the squire to hold up the suitcase once more while she made sure that she had not left most of it behind. She held it up for the audience's inspection. They looked at it with expectation while she consulted a label which provided a significant percentage of the object's substance.

'This is . . . er . . . a . . . Fifi.' She looked hopefully at the spectators who did not seem to be much the wiser. She correctly deduced that 'Fifi' was not a term the local males normally applied to anything in particular and re-consulted the label.

'Well, what does it say?' yelled Kelvin.

' "Fifi. Machine washable," ' replied Helga unhelpfully. 'I think it must be a *cache-sexe*.'

'What's a *cache-sexe*?' asked Bill.

Helga looked round the room for help. It can surely have not been because she felt embarrassed but because her command of the less-used nooks and crannies of the English language was not extensive. Everyone looked at Malcolm, a man with a degree, as the obvious person to supply the needed information.

'It's a sort of lady's jockstrap,' supplied Malcolm, reddening slightly under the warm gaze of so many pairs of eyes. The eyes shifted back to the *cache-sexe*.

'How do you wear it?' asked Bill. Helga gave him a quizzical look, but it was obviously a genuine request for knowledge. She turned it over carefully in her hand and a couple of strands of satin fell away from it. 'Ah! I have it now. You tie it on like this.' She tied it on like that, unfortunately over the top of her trousers, but the spectators got the general idea clearly enough as she swivelled her hips from side to side so that everyone could see. She clicked her fingers to break the squire out of his trance and he lifted up the suitcase from which she extracted the catalogue. 'A Fifi costs £2.35. Does anyone want to buy one?' She looked at the catalogue again. 'They only come in one size.'

'Well, they would, wouldn't they?' said the commander reasonably.

Nobody wanted a Fifi, so Helga took it off and rummaged around for something else. Her hand came up with a rat. She screamed and dropped it back into the suitcase. If it was a rat, it seemed to be dead and so Helga gingerly prodded it to ensure that it remained comatose and picked it up again between finger and thumb. Her face cleared. 'Ah! It is another *cache-sexe*.' She looked at the label. 'This one is called "Pussy".'

The commander's nose wrinkled in distaste. 'That's not very subtle.'

'I doubt if one can expect all that much subtlety in this sort of situation,' said Ivor.

'I suppose not.' Nobody wanted to buy a Pussy, nor a Cancan nor the rather bizarrely named Margery which was somewhat shocking since it had a hole where one would have thought its wearer would least have wanted one. Kelvin had had enough.

'Let's have something more exciting than all these hankies,' he said loudly. Everyone seemed to be in agreement, especially Helga, so she burrowed further down into the suitcase and came up with something more substantial. This was a nightie – even Kelvin recognized it as such – but it was not the sort of nightie that was donned by the average farmer's wife after she had slipped off her Wellington boots beside the bed and groped beneath the pillow. This one was a bright scarlet, foaming with lace of the same colour, with filmy net over the parts where the interesting bits were most likely to be. This was more like it and there was a gasp of appreciation from the voyeurs.

'Coo!' said Kelvin almost involuntarily. 'I wouldn't mind one of those.'

Helga looked at him critically and then back at the

garment. 'It would not really suit you, Kelvin dear. It would clash with your complexion.'

'I didn't mean I would want it for myself,' said Kelvin. 'I mean, it's for a lady, isn't it? Not for the likes of me.'

'I wouldn't be in too much of a hurry to give a thing like that to a lady, Kelvin,' said the commander. 'But if you didn't want it for yourself, who was it for? Nellie?'

Kelvin blushed deeply.

'Poor Kelvin,' said Helga sympathetically. 'Leave the poor man alone. It is not fair to mock him for being romantic.'

Kelvin blushed even deeper. 'I'm not romantic,' he protested.

Nobody but Helga was willing to argue with him. He was about as romantic as a haddock but she persuaded him to lash out nearly £10 on the nightie which gave all present considerable food for thought. Extracting money from Kelvin was more difficult than passing a camel through the eye of a needle, so his need of such a garment must have been very great.

Helga continued to burrow deep into the suitcase. Underneath the topsoil of filmy negligees and g-strings, she discovered a mysterious stratum of mock-leather boxes. With the triumphant air of one who has uncovered a nugget of gold in the gravel of a Yukon river bed, she freed one from the clinging embrace of rayon, satin and nylon that crackled and flashed as it reluctantly gave it up. It had two words emblazoned in gold on its lid. 'Triple orgasm,' Helga read out. There was a suck of indrawn breath from the audience. This was a bit more like it. It must contain one hell of a pair of knickers. Helga opened the box and held it up to the audience to show its contents nestling in a cocoon of red plastic. It contained four mysterious pink objects and an ordinary torch battery. There was a buzz of speculation as to what their purpose could be. The commander did his best to look knowing as he had his reputation as an international sexual sophisticate to maintain, but everyone else, including Helga who might have been expected to have experience of most aspects of love making, looked stumped. Helga picked up the leaflet which was enclosed and read it out to the respectful silence.

' "A titillating trio of vibrating egg for her, ring for him and porator for both." ' Her voice ended on a puzzled note and she looked doubtfully back at the contents of the box. 'I do not understand,' she said. 'What, for instance, is this word "porator"?' She looked round the room to a succession of blank gazes. 'Does anyone know?'

The squire, beneath his suitcase, spoke up. 'There's a dictionary behind Ivor in the bookshelf.' It was a big dictionary too. One that had provided food for bookworms as well as thought down the century since it had been published, but the word was not in it.

Kelvin was worried about something else. 'Why should her want a vibrating egg?'

The commander was at least up to that question. A group of youths edged closer to share in the enlightenment. 'It's for a woman to put inside herself and then it vibrates.'

Kelvin looked puzzled. 'What's the point of that? And why should it be shaped like an egg?'

'The vibration is stimulating,' explained the commander carefully, 'although I've no idea why they should make it egg-shaped.'

'It might do something for a hen, I suppose,' said Kelvin.

Helga was removing the items from their box for closer examination. The ring was obviously the ring. There was a rocket-shaped object which was presumably the porator, but what earthly use it might be to both parties was not clear, and the egg was fixed with a piece of string to an object that looked vaguely like a baby's dummy. She looked baffled. 'Does anyone want to buy these? They are only £12.50?' There was a stony silence. Helga sighed. 'Perhaps we ought to go and ask Lesley what these things are for.'

The box was replaced and Helga rummaged around for something else. This time she came upon a small bottle which she held up for all to see.

'And the next object is a bottle. A bottle,' murmured the commander.

Helga squinted at the label. ' "Booby drops?" ' she said, looking round with a wild surmise.

'Keep reading,' said the commander.

She kept reading in tones of increasing incredulity. ' "Booby drops – a drop rubbed into the nipples makes each one a sucker's paradise. Banana, chocolate or strawberry flavours." ' She paused. 'I think that is the most disgusting thing I have ever heard.'

Her audience was not enjoying it very much either. They had come round for a bit of a laugh, but were finding that there was precious little fun to be found. They practised on the craggy uplands of sexual experience and they were finding the steamier swamps of the lowlands rather unsettling and faintly obscene. Helga next came out with a bewildering array of vibrators. Her audience had heard of those and were rather shocked at their graphic modelling. When she came out with Maximum Big Man Cream – an eight-week course for a large, firm, full organ – there were some who felt that a gross of jars might be no bad thing, judging by the size of some of the vibrators, but Helga sampled it by tongue and said that it was nothing more than cold cream.

Then came an array of rubber goodies – each looking more like a medieval torture implement than the last. Somehow the humour of the situation was being lost. Helga succeeded in extracting some money from people when some of the joke items came up, but her disgust tended to show through. Sales were not helped when the commander pointed out that the surprise element of most of the jokes would be lost, since most potential recipients were already present in the room. The party closed with a short speech of thanks from Ivor who did not seem to be much happier than anyone else and the men of the village, rather chastened, trooped out of the room.

In the hall, the women were gathered for their party. There was a vain attempt by some of their spouses to pull them away from the forthcoming experience but they had little success as the wives had been stoking up in the pub beforehand and were in the right sort of mood to enjoy themselves. Most of the men went back to the pub to have a consoling drink.

'None of the stuff was really shocking,' Bill said, once he had fitted his haunches into the depression that he had made on his stool down the years and had a pint nestling cosily inside his hand. 'But a lot of it was rather silly.'

'I've a feeling that much of it might have been shocking if we could have only worked out what it was all supposed to be,' contributed Ivor. 'I did quite like Kelvin's nightie, all the same.'

'Did you buy anything?' asked Kelvin.

'Yes,' replied Ivor rather hesitantly.

'Well, let's have a look, then,' said Kelvin.

Sheepishly Ivor pulled out from his pocket a flimsy-looking rubber ball which was subjected to a silent scrutiny.

'It doesn't seem to be very much,' said Kelvin. 'What's it for?'

'It's not actually for anything,' replied Ivor.

'You must have spent good money on it, so what does it do?'

'You squeeze it,' said Ivor.

'Ah!' said the commander, 'you squeeze it. How fascinating! I didn't see Helga hold up that.'

'No, she didn't, actually.' Ivor made to put the object back in his pocket but his wrist was held by the commander.

'OK,' the commander said, 'so you squeeze it. Then what happens?'

'Nothing very much.'

'I know!' cried Kelvin. 'He's got one of those inflatable women there. I've heard about them, but I didn't see any up at the manor. I was rather looking forward to seeing some . . . so long as they were nice and big.'

'It's got to be a very small inflatable woman that Ivor's got there,' said the commander, looking down at the object in Ivor's hand. 'Squeeze it.' Ivor reluctantly did as he was bade and, before the wondering gaze of the barflies, the thing obligingly produced a 6-inch erection: pink, with a red tip. 'Good God!' said the commander. 'You went and spent your money on a thing like that?'

'I thought it was rather fun,' replied Ivor defensively. 'It only cost £2.50.'

The commander turned sadly back to the bar. 'Think of the drinks you could have bought me for £2.50.'

'But it was in aid of the church clock,' said Ivor.

The pub sat in morose silence for some time, reflecting on the events of the evening. 'I don't reckon that it was a good idea letting our women see some of that sort of stuff,' announced Kelvin.

'You could be right,' said Bill, 'but it's too late to worry about it now.' He glanced at his watch. 'It'll probably soon be over anyway.'

Kelvin was not to be mollified. 'I don't know what my Prudence will make of it at all,' he said with a shake of his head.'

'I think she'll be all right,' reassured Bill. In the silence of the bar, we sat and thought of Prudence. She was Kelvin's only child and was agreed to be a good worker. This was the highest accolade that could be bestowed by the older generation. The trouble was that times had changed and such a virtue was no longer appreciated as it had been in the old days. Modern youth liked pretty faces and sweet natures in their girlfriends and Prudence had neither, so much so that even her agricultural potential as sole heir to Kelvin's stretch of England had been insufficient to tempt any suitors when she had been in her prime a decade earlier. The fact that her husband would have had to put up with Kelvin as a father-in-law may well have had some bearing on her remaining in spinsterhood.

Suddenly the latch clicked and the pub door was flung open with a crash to admit Lindy with a couple of other women and a blast of cold air which tore into the rather pleasant fug that had built up. They were in high spirits. '£350!' exulted Lindy.

'What!' exclaimed Bill.

'Yes. You useless men could only raise £50 amongst you. It's just as well you had us to rely on.'

'How come you made so much?' asked Ivor.

'We brought in Lesley. She is rather nice, you know, and she explained what everything was while Helga modelled it.'

'Oh no,' groaned the commander. 'Why couldn't she have done that for us?'

'It was thanks to the squire's wife,' explained Lindy. 'She took one sip of the wine and brought out some of her own instead. We all got rather merry.' She confirmed this with a belch and a shriek of laughter.

'Who bought what?' asked Ivor with interest.

'Ah! That would be telling. I'm sure you'll find out in good time.' That did nothing to relieve the faint air of apprehension among the assembled males.

'Is my Prudence all right?' asked Kelvin.

'Prudence? She had a whale of a time. She bought two vibrators and a pot of bust-enlarging cream.'

'Prudence!' gasped Kelvin. 'She can't have done!'

'She damn well did. Prudence has a secret life, you can be sure of that, Kelvin.'

Prudence's was the only purchase that ever became public knowledge. There were certainly some very tired and some very thoughtful men around the village for the next week or two, but they were too secretive ever to compare notes.

The church clock had been ticking away for some weeks, just like it always had done, before the subject of the party came up in the pub again. It was triggered by Helga saying that she had had a letter from Lesley. Kelvin had smiled a slow smile. 'Do you remember those things that Prudence bought at he party?' Everybody did. 'The bust cream was useless. She wanted it to put on the udders of the cows and nothing happened at all.'

After a pause, Ivor delicately prompted him: 'And the vibrators?'

'Ah, now they were different. Very useful, they were.'

'In what way?' asked Ivor, surprised.

Kelvin looked at him craftily. 'I don't think I ought to tell you. It wasn't what you think. She's a sharp maid, my Prudence.'

'Oh, go on,' cajoled Bill, his curiosity now aroused. 'We'll keep it a secret.'

'You've got to promise, mind. And buy me a drink if you want to copy the idea.'

'We promise!' chorused those present.

'All right, then. Prudence wanted those vibrators for the two great water troughs in my yard, the ones that always freeze over. She's wired them to the mains through transformers and every time it looks like being frosty she puts them on and they jiggle the surface of the water and stop it freezing. They work a real treat.' Kelvin looked smugly round the awe-struck faces.

'She's no fool, your Prudence,' said Bill eventually.

'Cheap-rate electrics too,' said Kelvin. 'Giving you lot the idea is surely worth a pint, isn't it?'

'What'll you have, Kelvin?' asked Ivor.

Chapter Two

THERE IS fishing and fishing. The sport enjoyed in the north of Scotland, where you stand in your waders watching the salmon queue up to take your flies while some wise gillie drivels on in the background about water conditions and passes round flasks of whisky, is not common. The great majority of anglers in this country go in for coarse fishing where they chuck bits of bread and maggots into scummy water in the hope of catching fish with names like tench, carp, gudgeon, rudd, roach, chub or perch, all of which sound like the noises made by a rugby team regurgitating their beer and curry after an evening spent celebrating a win.

Fishing round the village, while not coarse, could scarcely be described as fine. The river and its many tributaries were certainly full of trout and even the odd salmon, but the snag was that there were so many trout that any fly foolish enough to land on the surface of the water would be torn fin from fin by a pack of starving fish. Anglers had to pull out a dozen or so before they could be sure that they would fill up an empty pilchard tin. It was game fishing, but a far cry from the sport to be found on the Dee, Don or Spey.

It was made even more suspect by the process of battery-rearing trout. After dairying and sheep rearing, one of the biggest industries in the area was fish farming. Great stewponds full of fat rainbows dotted the landscape, marked by the crowds of wheeling herons and cormorants above them like the vultures of Africa above a dead elephant, waiting for the farmer and his shotgun to go away so that they could drop down and feast themselves on this remarkable avian delicatessen.

Curiously, the greatest predator of the fish farms, apart from the epidemics which swept through them like bubonic plague through the ghettoes of medieval Europe, was the wren. It was so small that virtually no chicken wire could keep it out and it foraged round the hatchery trays, rearing four or five broods a year on the fry.

The fish could be harvested in a variety of ways. Almost everyone who cultivated fish let out rod space to the tourists. They were very useful since their presence kept the other predators at bay. If a pond were lined with villainously camouflaged fishermen from Brum and Leeds, all the other fish thieves made themselves scarce. They were not only useful as scarecrows, these fishermen, but they were profitable in themselves. They could be hit for a tenner a day for the privilege of standing by one of the ponds and charged per liveweight pound for everything they caught at a price comfortably above that which a fishmonger dared to ask.

The illusion of man-the-hunter was sometimes rather difficult to achieve on the stewponds. Game fishing, after all, is supposed to be a testing battle of wits between man and fish, and the denizens of these ponds were used to coming to the bank to beg for their food a couple of times a day all of their lives. It could be rather embarrassing when a newly arrived angler, creeping along behind bushes so that he would not frighten the fish on his way to a good position, was followed down the bank by hordes of voracious trout, most of which were poking their heads out of the water or blowing bubbles at the unfortunate man so that they could get his attention long enough to ensure that he would chuck his bait at them and not their neighbours. Fortunately, the type of fisherman who frequented the stewponds knew no better. He might be equipped with £1000's worth of rods, nets and tackle and throw flies constructed from entire macaws at the fish, but the fine art of river fishing was way beyond his ken. Something fat and simple that jumped on to his hook and made him feel like a cross between Captain Ahab and the last of the Mohicans was what he was about.

As well as the rivers and ponds, there were a couple of lakes in the neighbourhood. Historically, water had never been in short supply for the local population. Enough came down from the sky and occasionally bulged out of the rivers, drowning large tracts of the landscape, to provide ample for the needs of the people and the farms round about. But the summer millions who came down were something new. Their thirsts had to be satisfied somehow and two reservoirs had been built. One lay about a dozen miles outside the village where a valley had been blocked by a mighty curtain of concrete, backing up the rather insignificant river that had flowed through it until it became a dozen square miles of water that reacted violently to the constant and unpredictable moorland winds by throwing up waves which broke strongly on the cow pastures of the shore. It was still a curious half-world between water and land. Lanes and barbed-wire fences marched solemnly into the water to disappear beneath the waves and emerge on the opposite bank half a mile away.

The water was still an alien presence, grafted on to an ancient landscape. There was no beach, just a lifeless fringe of mud where the waves had pounded at the turf and drowned the grass. Forests still poked above the water, providing perches for cormorants rather than wood pigeons and, in the height of the tourist summer, drowned farms complete with their modern concrete single-span buildings still rose, dripping, from the lake. Just as the land seemed uneasy with its new neighbour, the water itself looked unused to its surroundings. No islands emerged to give it substance. No reeds fringed it to give it definition. No houses clustered on its banks or poked their piers and jetties out into it. It looked no more natural than water in a bath.

This bleak prospect had some use. The fish farmers found a splendid new market as the water authority bought from them scores of thousands of trout a year for release into the lake: they had created one of the largest stewponds in the country and, with 15 miles of shoreline, the tourists and their tackle could sometimes appear to be shoulder to shoulder round its circumference. The farmers whose land had been swallowed up found these trout something of a comfort. It was very easy to leave nets or baited traps moored to one of their old hedgerows and keep their freezers well stocked. There was a warden whose job it was to prevent this sort of thing, but he was a refugee from a car factory in the Midlands who had no hope of curtailing the activities of these sly countrymen with a lifetime of experience to assist them, who had passed the halycon days of their youth poaching under the noses of gamekeepers.

After a year or two of its existence, the reservoir began to be developed. A yacht club and a windsurfing centre were built and the pancake of water became populated by capsized dinghies and windsurfers, shivering in their wetsuits as they scudded before the gales. The water authority built a jetty a tied a dozen rowing boats to it which were let out to the fishermen. They organized fishing festivals and competitions that attracted people from hundreds of miles away. Although the reservoir was some distance from the village, this was right out on an unpopulated part of the moor and so it was the nearest local conurbation, if a village of two or three hundred people could be described as such.

In spite of this new addition to the amenities of the area, nobody from the village used to visit it until the commander decided that this was something that ought to be rectified. His birthday was coming up, he went around telling people, and he thought it would be a good idea to organize a party for all his friends. There was some reservation about this. Although the commander had been in the village for five years and had managed to establish himself firmly as an amiable eccentric in the most respectable rural tradition, there still lingered memories of his arrival. For a month he had been insufferable. He had gone round in a pair of immaculate cavalry twills, trying to bully and cajole the villagers into running their lives and affairs in ways that he considered efficient. He had been broken, of course, by the enormous weight of tradition and apathy, but not before he had made himself thoroughly unpopular and it had taken a couple of years of suspicious observation to make sure that he really had become a harmless drunk before the villagers were prepared to take him to their collective bosom. Now here he was trying to organize everyone again.

'I would like to take all my friends up to the reservoir on Saturday so that we can do some fishing and have a barbecue,' he announced in the pub.

Lindy looked over with interest. 'That sounds fun. Can I bring the family?'

'Certainly,' said the commander. 'How about you, Kelvin? Will you come and bring Prudence as well?'

'Why?' asked Kelvin. Since he never did anything without a selfish motive, he naturally assumed that everyone else was the same.

'Why? I thought she might enjoy it. Heaven knows, she doesn't appear to get much chance to enjoy herself.'

On the rare occasions when Prudence came to the village to collect her father's pension from the post office, she would hurry through with her eyes averted so as to avoid the agonies of trying to overcome her shyness to make conversation.

'No, I wasn't thinking about Prudence—'

'Surprise, surprise,' murmured Lindy.

'— I was wanting to know why *I* should come.'

The commander raised his eyebrows in surprise at the question. 'Because I'm inviting you, of course.'

'Will it cost me anything?' The rest of the pub was listening with close attention. Kelvin, with his rhino-like skin, was putting all the questions that the rest were too polite to state out loud and could only wonder about.

'Of course it won't cost you anything,' snapped the commander indignantly. 'It's going to be my birthday party.'

'Will I have to do any work?'

'Look,' said the commander in exasperation. 'All I'm doing is asking you to come to a party. I'm not asking you to interview me.'

'Hmm,' ruminated Kelvin, 'it doesn't sound much like a party to me. Up at the reservoir. Parties are things that you have at home in the evening. Not miles away and during the day.'

'Well, I'm sorry,' said the commander. 'I thought it might

be a bit different and could be fun. You don't have to come.'

'I didn't say that I wouldn't come,' said Kelvin hurriedly. 'I just wanted to know what it would be like.'

'Well,' said the commander, 'I thought that a couple of dozen or so of us could go up there and take out a few boats and do some fishing and then, if it's a nice day, we might go over to that little corner on the south side that was so difficult to get to before and have a barbecue.'

'What about drink, though? Would you be expecting guests to provide their own drink?'

'Certainly not,' said the commander hurriedly. While a few connoisseurs like Dennis would inevitably turn up with their whisky – in Dennis's case, safely screwed into a flash in his pocket – the main bulk of them would bring brews made from potato peelings, rhubarb, and the less poisonous of the native wild flowers. This would lead to a ghastly unbalanced affair, during the first half-hour of which guests consumed as much as possible of the drinkable foreign wines and all the spirits in the hope that they would be inebriated enough not to mind when the approaching drought forced them to move on to the drink that they had brought themselves. On one memorable occasion, the vicar, who had just come back from a duty-free excursion to Boulogne, had provided so much free good wine that the party he gave had to finish abruptly after an hour as most of the guests were too helplessly drunk to participate any further.

'No?' said Kelvin, his eyes gleaming. 'You mean you will provide all the drink yourself?'

'Yes,' said the commander.

There was a sharp intake of breath from Jimmy and the ever-present cigarette that dangled from his withered lips was almost sucked back into his mouth. He broke into a fit of coughing before noisily spitting on to his shoe. Helga had stopped him from spitting on the pub floor but was unable to stop him spitting. 'You'll pay for proper drink for everybody?' he asked incredulously. 'That'll cost a terrible amount of money.'

'I've just had a win on a horse,' said the commander.

'Balls!' said Bill. 'You don't know one end of a horse from another, and anyway you never bet.'

The commander looked pained. 'If you must know, my old nanny, who's now in her eighties, send me £200 for my birthday.'

'And you took it?' said Dennis disapprovingly. He was a farmer of sorts, but enough of a gentleman farmer to have been reared by a nanny as well. 'You'd deprive someone like that of £200? The poor old thing is probably senile and didn't know what she was doing.'

'You think I ought to send it back?' asked the commander. 'I must say that when I first opened the letter and saw the cheque, I did wonder if she might have made a mistake. But it didn't bounce.'

'Course you shouldn't send it back,' said Bill, worried at the prospect of losing an afternoon's free boozing. 'That would make the poor old thing very unhappy.'

'Well, she was an employee of my parents. And now she has only a tiny pension to keep her going.'

'All the more reason why you should not give the money back,' said Bill reassuringly. 'She'd be too proud to take it, quite apart from thinking that the reason you didn't want it was that it came from her and that her money wasn't good enough for you.'

'That's a very good point,' said the commander thoughtfully. 'That's the reason I didn't return the cheque straight away.'

Dennis snorted in derision.

'You don't have to come to the party if your conscience is bothering you,' said Bill, rounding on him.

Dennis held up his hands placatingly. 'I didn't say anything.'

'I didn't say you did say anything,' replied Bill. 'But I didn't say you didn't.'

'Shut up, you two,' said Lindy. 'Commander, I think your idea for a party is quite splendid.'

'I'll feel just like a bloody tourist,' muttered Kelvin.

On the appointed day, there were a full two dozen villagers mustered in the car park by the reservoir. In a curious reversal of the usual roles, the tourists looked like countrymen and vice versa. All the Midlands fishermen had their heads bowed down under the weight of the fishing flies in their hats, while the browns of their thick tweeds and shiny anoraks made them look like mobile cowpats as they trudged past, festooned with rods, tackle pouches and landing nets, towards their patch of reservoir bank. They gazed with contempt upon the squire's long khaki shorts and the primitive fishing implements that were carried by the locals.

The commander had reserved three boats for the day. The idea was that we should row across the water to the picnic spot and then allow those who wished to fish to fish and those who wished to lie around in the sunshine and get drunk to do just that. There was a knot of disgruntled anglers on the jetty, the end of which was a prime fishing position, and they saw no reason why they should have to stop their frantic casting to permit access to the craft. Kelvin, playing the special constable, cleared the fishermen away, however, and we loaded the boats with plastic containers of cider and the little

mummified bodies of pheasants provided from the commander's larder, still exuding their freezer chill through their plastic cocoons. It was one of those lovely summer days without a breath of wind to stir the hot air with the water mercury-still except where rings from the rising trout spread out across the surface.

The commander took charge of the flotilla, giving land lubbers a quick course in oarsmanship, passing out instructions forbidding passengers to stand up and checking who might be the swimmers in case anyone fell overboard. With the line of fishermen on either side of the jetty looking contemptuously on, the party set off. The commander was admiral of the fleet with the booze safely stacked in the bilges of his vessel. Lindy was in charge of the food and number two boat which was populated with the most sensible and cautious members of the party – almost all women – who had chosen to sail with the captain in whom they might have the greatest degree of confidence.

The heavy mob was under the charge of Dennis. Dennis had been appointed to the job when he had told the commander that he had once seriously thought of taking up rowing when he had been at school, but his boat was only a few yards off the jetty when it became apparent that he had not thought about it too deeply. The boats could carry eight people apiece and Ivor and Keith had been appointed to take first stint at the oars.

'Where's the rudder?' demanded Dennis, looking around the stern where he had seated himself.

'I don't think there is one,' replied Ivor, who had a sheen of sweat on his face after half a dozen strokes.

'Of course there must be a rudder. All boats have rudders, otherwise you can't steer,' retorted Dennis scornfully.

'They don't seem to have one on the other boats', said Keith.

Dennis's boat was supposed to be following in their wake, but it was already 20 yards behind and beginning to slew to port, enabling Keith to have an unimpeded view.

'I feel sick,' said Jimmy.

'Don't be so bloody silly. You can't possibly feel sick. You'd be as likely to feel sick in your bath,' said Kelvin. 'Mind you, perhaps you do feel sick in the bath, which is why you never have one.'

Jimmy was undoubtedly turning green. 'I think I'm going to be sick,' he insisted.

'Don't worry. You won't be,' reassured Ivor, whose rowing position just in front of Jimmy made him extremely vulnerable.

'How do you know?' asked Jimmy.

'Well, we're on a lake and you don't get lake-sick. There's no such thing. You can only get sea-sick, so you're bound to be all right because we're not at sea.'

Jimmy brightened immediately. 'I didn't think of that. So I can't be feeling sick at all, can I?'

'That's right,' said Ivor.

'The man's a bloody moron,' muttered Kelvin. The boat had now travelled in an almost complete circle and was heading back towards the jetty. 'I think you'd better do something, Dennis,' continued Kelvin, 'otherwise we're going to have a crash.'

Dennis had been peering down into the water over the back of the boat, trying to find the rudder, and he raised his head to look at the jetty and the interested bunch of fishermen who had been following our progress. 'Quite right. Ship oars!'

Keith gnawed his moustache worriedly as he caught a crab. 'What does that mean?'

'It means stop rowing,' said Ivor.

Keith dug his oar into the water and the boat lurched away from the jetty round the axis of his oar.

'That's it!' exclaimed Dennis. 'I remember now. You steer by pulling harder on one oar or the other.'

'You could always take another oar and use that as the rudder.'

'That's an excellent idea! Is there a spare oar lying around?'

We all looked round the boat and under the seats but there was no spare oar.

'Ask one of the fishermen to chuck one over from another of the boats.' They were close enough to the jetty to allow the

Kelvin looked at him in irritation. 'You can't make a decent bang with a newspaper. Use your initiative, man. They had a drum in the film. Find something like a drumstick.'

'Has anybody got a drumstick?' asked Jimmy, plaintively.

'Use your knuckles,' said Kelvin. 'Now, everybody ready? Right Jimmy, bang!'

The oars dipped as Jimmy banged. They waited for the next bang but it did not come. They looked round to see Jimmy rocking on his seat, moaning as blood trickled down his fist.

'For Christ's sake!' yelled Kelvin, Fletcher Christianing away. 'Bang, you daft old goat!'

'I've hurt my hand, Kelvin,' moaned Jimmy.

'Well, use the other one, then.'

'But if I hurt that, I won't be able to open any bottles.'

'Why don't you just say "bang"?' suggested Ivor.

'That's a good idea,' agreed Kelvin.

So, with Jimmy saying 'bang', we slowly tacked our way across to the other side of the reservoir.

By the time our boat finally grounded on the muddy shore, the commander and the others were already making camp. The favoured spot was the unflooded half of a small clearing that had been in the middle of a rather scrubby coniferous plantation, the water side of which had been felled before it had been flooded. The brambles now grew thick throughout and, although the commander had had sufficient sense to requisition a couple of scythes, there was a rather rebellious group standing on the shore while they waited for space to be created in which they could set up the fire and lay out the chairs. It looked wise to avoid the area for a half-hour or so.

'We'll go and get some fish,' said Kelvin, after surveying the scene. 'We'll see you back in an hour.'

'Would you like a few pigeons?' Dave asked the harassed commander.

'Yes, anything would be useful. Before you go fishing, Kelvin, it would be a help if you could get the fire lit.'

Dave was a country boyo through and through. Many of the young round about were interested only in sex, motor bikes and space-invader machines and hankered for the low city life, but Dave had fully imbibed the old-fashioned lore of his ancestors and found his pleasures in watching deer and poaching pheasants and fish. He had once come out of a local fish farm with 60lb of prime trout in response to a dare. This particular farm had been established by a foreigner from up country somewhere. He was utterly paranoid about poaching, but there had not been enough of a challenge to interest the locals until he had thrown down the gauntlet by surrounding his ponds with chain-link fencing and releasing a couple of homicidal Alsatians to roam around inside looking for intruders whom they could tear to pieces. Dave had picked up the gauntlet. He borrowed a bitch that was on heat, cut a hole in the fence to push her through and, while the guard dogs had the time of their frustrated lives, he leisurely filled a couple of fertilizer sacks with fish. Percy, our local policeman, had then advised the farmer to remove all his poaching deterrent and Dave, and others like him, had not bothered to go back.

Watching Dave catching pigeons for the barbecue without a gun was likely to be educational, so I tagged along as he went off into the larches behind the clearing.

'How many pigeons do you think the commander would like?' he asked.

'I should think half a dozen would be ample,' I said. 'After all, he's got all those pheasants and Kelvin and his chums might catch a few fish.'

'I suppose so. Let's make it eight just to be on the safe side.'

'You seem to find pigeon catching very easy,' I remarked as we came to a stop beneath a tree.

'Yeah. I did this wood a few weeks ago. I think I've got twenty-odd pigeons here. There are a couple in this tree.'

'How do you know?'

'I marked it,' he said, pointing to a small cross that had been cut into the bark at ground level. He looked measuringly at the tree and swiftly clambered up into the foliage. There was the sound of flapping above and he re-appeared a minute or two later, carrying a couple of large plump pigeons. It might have been understandable if they had been unfledged young, but these were fully adult. It was like a conjuring trick.

'How on earth did you manage that?' I asked, astounded.

Dave was always delightfully willing to share the secrets of his skills with anyone who seemed interested, although usually they were none the wiser after his explanation.

'What you do,' explained Dave, 'is go round the wood in early summer and look for pigeon nests. When you find one, you just climb up to it and tie a bit of fishing line to the leg of one of the squabs. Then you thread it through the bottom of the nest and tie it to a branch underneath. It's simple really. The bird can't fly away and the parents will keep feeding it until it leaves the nest, which it can't do. So it just gets fatter and fatter until you feel like a pigeon for supper and you go and pick it up.'

'Coo!' I said, overwhelmed by the simple efficiency of the scheme.

'The only thing that's a bit difficult is making sure that you give the bird the right amount of slack. Too much and it will topple out of the nest and hang upside down until it dies, and too little and it won't get enough exercise. I've found that it helps if it can flap its wings properly. It builds up the breast and it doesn't get tough. Hold these, will you?'

I took the two pigeons while Dave shinned up another tree and came down with another one. 'You can't help feeling a bit sorry for the birds,' he continued, after he had neatly wrung the neck of his latest acquisition. 'But I don't suppose it's much worse than being a chicken in a battery cage. At least they have a view to look at.'

'That's true.' I had lived in the country long enough to realize that a tender conscience is a city luxury which has to be discarded once one gets beyond the 30 mph limits.

'It keeps the population of pigeons down, you know.'

'How's that?'

'There's no point in shooting up the nests because the adults just go and start another clutch. But this way they keep on feeding their young in the nests and so don't lay again.'

'I see.' By this time we had eight pigeons and were moving

back through the wood towards the clearing. 'How many birds have you got altogether?'

'I didn't do very many this year. I've got about seventy left.'

'That's not bad.'

'I've had a couple of hundred in other years.'

It was a beautiful scheme. If Dave had reared poultry himself, he would have had to provide them with housing and

feed and they would probably die of disease if they were given a chance. This way, he only needed a few lengths of fishing line and the mother birds fed his stock for nothing and looked after them for him if he went away.

We returned to the clearing. The barbecue was set in an old disc of a harrow that was propped up on some chicken wire over the fire. Kelvin, in charge of the fire, had obviously had some difficulty in getting it lit as there was an old tyre blazing merrily away underneath, wreathing black smoke over the chilled lumps of pheasant above and then on into the sky, filling the surrounding air with the stench of rubber. There was a furious altercation going on between himself and Lindy, in charge of the cooking.

'How the hell am I supposed to cook on top of that?' she demanded.

'If you're afraid of the heat, I can put things on for you.'

'Don't be stupid. It's not the heat I'm worried about, it's the smoke. It's going to make everything taste of burning rubber.'

'Just like your home cooking!' Kelvin retired to the shade of a tree with one of Dennis's personal bottles of whisky, muttering and rubbing his skull, off which one of the frozen pheasants had bounced.

The commander looked over in irritation. 'Instead of doing nothing, Kelvin, it would be a big help if you would take your boat out and catch some fish. I thought you said that's what you were going to do.'

Because the majority of the Establishment of the village had come out for the day, the unprecedented step of buying a fishing permit had been taken. Ivor had decided that it would have been too embarrassing for so many respectable citizens to risk being caught without the necessary authorization.

Kelvin got to his feet and wandered to the shore. 'Who's nicked the boat?' he demanded.

'What are you talking about?' asked the commander, who was concentrating on removing the harrow disc from the fire without burning his fingers so that he could give it a scrub and to get rid of the rubber deposits.

'The boat we came over in. It's not here.'

The commander came the few yards down to the shore, looking up and down the beach. 'It must have drifted off.'

'It can't have done. I tied it up.'

'What did you fasten her to?'

'There was a bit of wood in the water. I tied it to that.'

The commander gave Kelvin a withering look. 'You still have the power to surprise me, Kelvin. Your boat and its anchor are both floating down the lake, over there.' He indicated the craft, which was 100 yards away and about 10 yards out from the shore. 'I suggest you go and retrieve it.'

'I don't see why it has to be me who goes,' objected Kelvin.

'I can think of several reasons why it should be you,' replied the commander. 'For a start, you're the only person who's doing nothing round here. Secondly, it's you who needs the boat to go fishing. And thirdly, you were the pillock who tied the boat to a floating branch!'

'You could go and I could clean that there disc,' said Kelvin.

'The final point is that the boat will eventually drift to the dam wall and over the slipway.'

'Tough,' said Kelvin, laconically.

'It will make it a long walk to get home,' said the commander mildly. 'And, of course, the boat was booked out in your name, so you will be liable for any damage that is caused to it. I must get back to my cooking.' The commander knew when he had delivered a clincher, and returned to his scrubbing without a further glance at Kelvin. The latter stared at the commander's unresponsive back in baffled frustration, uttered a few swear words and plodded off down the shoreline. The commander left his task and called the rest of us over: 'Watch Kelvin. It might be fun.'

We watched Kelvin. It was fun. He reached the point opposite the slowly drifting boat and sat down to take off his shoes and socks. He took a long stick and paddled out into the water. He got about a quarter of the way before the water was lapping at his trousers so he retired to the shore and looked thoughtfully out at the boat. He threw a few stones out beyond it which had no discernible effect except to make the boat rock slightly and cause an ugly splintering sound when he misjudged his throw and one of them landed inside.

He then briefly disappeared into the trees that lined the shore and re-emerged without his trousers and waded out towards it. This time, he reached it. The water was just wetting his knickers when he made a last desperate lunge as a puff of breeze caught the boat and pulled it a few inches beyond his reach. There was a sigh of pleasure from the watchers as he measured his length in the water, then emerged, spluttering, to grab hold of the gunwales and drag it towards the shore. He retrieved his trousers, put them in the boat and paddled back along the edge of the lake, dragging the boat behind him.

'Bit wet, are you, Kelvin?' asked Jimmy.

Kelvin was not at his sunniest. 'Yes, I'm bloody wet. You knew this would happen, didn't you?' he said to the commander accusingly.

'How on earth could I know that you were going to fall over?' replied the commander. 'I have to admit that I did hope you would, and indeed I suspected you might, but I couldn't have known it.'

'You're laughing at me,' said Kelvin.

'Yes, but not out loud,' replied the commander. 'Why don't you go and do some fishing now?'

Kelvin did not feel like doing some fishing. He had a deep aversion to immersing his body in water and felt the need to appropriate one of Dennis's whisky bottles and go to sit under a nearby tree in order to recuperate. He took off his baggy grey underpants and strung them over a bush to dry, draping his nether regions in a towel. As the afternoon wore on, he became extremely drunk. This did not matter too much as everyone else became rather inebriated too, but Kelvin is one of those unfortunate people who become increasingly belligerent the more alcohol he consumes. He tried to pick a fight with Bill over a half-cooked pigeon and, when that failed, fell out with Mary Mowbray on the best way to break in a horse. Since Mary knew her horses better than her own children and Kelvin hadn't been near one since he bought a tractor for the first time and stopped using shires, it was felt to be a little unreasonable.

It was a damn good party and it was past 8pm and the light was beginning to fade when we decided that it was time to wend our way homeward. The midges were out and, after a few bites of the over-the-limit blood that was all that there was available, they were kamikaze-ing into the fire and drowning themselves in beer glasses as they hiccuped their way from target to target. Even the trout that had been skulking in the cool depths during the heat of the day were now splashing about on the surface like dolphins, and the excited voices of the professional fishermen that carried for hundreds of yards across the still surface of the water showed that some were letting themselves in for large bills on their return to the control hut with its set of scales, across which tons of slippery, pellet-fed corpses were weighed each year.

While the rest of us cleared up the debris, Kelvin, who had been wandering round like a Roman senator in his towel toga, retired behind a bush to replace his pants and clothes. He was incapable of doing anything low-key which meant that Mandy, Keith's formidable wife, was called over to pass him his pants from their make-shift line as he had forgotten to take them with him.

'Did you know your pants hummed, Kelvin?' she asked as she picked them up.

'What do you mean "hum"? They were clean this morning and they've just got soaking wet.'

'No, I didn't mean that they were dirty. They are humming, literally.'

The clearer-uppers paused in their work to lock into this bizarre conversation.

'Pants don't hum. They can't hum. Not even Kelvin's,' remarked the commander.

'Well, these do. Come and listen.'

While Kelvin spluttered in indignation from behind his bush, we dropped everything else and went over to form an fishermen to hear and one of them picked up an oar and hurled it, torpedo-like, towards the boat. It caught it amidships with a thud and Dennis gracefully retrieved it. We got underway again. Dennis stood up in the stern, dug his oar in and began to sing *O Sole Mio*. Kelvin and Malcolm joined the other two on the oars and the boat began to scud across the surface while Jimmy, his sickness now forgotten, dug out a fishing line and trailed it over the side with a large piece of cottonwool on the end concealing a hook. It was really very pleasant in the sunshine.

Then, halfway across, Kelvin staged a successful mutiny. As Dennis was taking a long swig from his hip flask, the boat veered violently off course, nearly tipping him overboard. It coincided with Jimmy hooking a whale. There was chaos. Keith and his fellow rower caught a crab which tumbled them off their seats while Jimmy, screeching with excitement, hauled powerfully on his line. As Dennis flailed his arms for balance, he lost his oar over the side and everyone began to shout at each other. Fortunately, Jimmy's whale turned out to be Dennis's oar, but by the time that we had sorted ourselves out, Kelvin had firmly pushed the protesting Dennis down to the other end of the boat. The crew looked at Kelvin with some apprehension.

'Right, you lot. Who remembers seeing the film *Ben Hur*?' There were murmurs of denial from everyone. 'You know. It was that one with the guy with a big chest and a chariot race.' This time there were a few nods of recognition. 'Right. Well, in *Ben Hur* they had a dirty great rowing boat with lots of people on the oars and there was a black man with a drum at the back who was banging away and they all had to row in time. So I'm going to get Jimmy to bang on the bottom of the boat and you lot on the oars have to keep in time with him.'

Jimmy struck up a nervous hand: 'What'll I bang with, Kelvin?'

'Anything you like, so long as it makes a noise. Now the rest of you sit completely still so that you don't rock the boat and we might get somewhere.'

'How about a newspaper?' asked Jimmy.

interested semi-circle round Mandy, ready to be serenaded by Kelvin's knickers.

'I can't hear anything,' said the commander.

Mandy lifted up the pants. 'They've stopped now.' She gave them a little shake. They hummed. 'There. Hear that!'

There was a murmur of appreciation from the pants' audience. Most were simply prepared to appreciate the entertainment but the commander was possessed of a spirit of scientific curiosity.

'How extraordinary! Let's have a look.' Kelvin had sat down behind his bush and was muttering and grumbling to himself that his protests about this violation of his garments had been ignored but, as the commander took his pants from Mandy's unprotesting hand and peered cautiously inside, he was moved to complain out loud again.

'Gimme back my clothes!'

'Shut up, Kelvin,' said the commander casually. 'You know, I can't understand this. There's absolutely nothing there. They seem to be perfectly ordinary underpants.' The pants gave lie to this statement by suddenly increasing the volume of their output before shutting up again. The commander turned them over in his hand. 'The only thing that can possibly explain it is that it is the elastic that is making the noise. It must be expanding or contracting and rubbing against the material. It must be something to do with getting wet.'

'Can I have my pants back now?' asked Kelvin plaintively.

The commander reluctantly handed them over the bush to him and returned to the task of clearing up. There was a sudden scream from behind Kelvin's bush and, as people turned to look, the pants sailed over the top, planed across towards them and landed on the ground.

'How very odd,' remarked the commander as Kelvin hopped about, gathering the towel round his loins, and proceeded to dance on top of the garment before sitting down beside them. 'Are you feeling all right?' he called.

'That was dreadful,' gasped the betowelled one.

'What was dreadful?'

'I was just pulling them up my legs when they started to hum again. I looked down and there was a dirty great hornet crawling out from that double bit of material which fits round the crotch.'

'Oh, I see! It must have hidden there when you put them on the bush to dry. It was obviously disturbed when Mandy picked them up. That makes sense. But there was no reason to dance on the poor thing. Hornets are placid insects and are becoming quite rare.'

Kelvin turned wild-eyed to the commander. 'Bugger the bloody hornet. Think what would have happened if it hadn't crawled out when it did.'

We thought and shuddered.

A hole was dug to bury the remains of the hornet, which Kelvin carefully extricated from his knickers, and the rest of the picnic debris, after which the boats were loaded up. Kelvin was well beyond the responsibilities of command and he was unceremoniously dumped in the stern of one of the craft as we tacked our way back across the breadth of the lake with the oarsmen spending as much time disentangling themselves from the bottom of the vessels after they had missed their strokes and fallen off the benches as actually propelling the boats forward. The evening was made hideous with drunken renderings of *Widecombe Fair*. At one point there was a loud splash and there was some discussion of the size of fish that could have made it. Jimmy had just decided on a shark when Ivor noticed something amiss.

'Where's Kelvin?' he asked. 'I thought he was in the front of our boat.'

The rowers looked round.

'Well, he's certainly not here. He must have gone in the other boat.'

'He must have done, I suppose. But it's funny, because I thought he came with us,' said Dennis.

'I thought so too,' said Jimmy. 'I remember trying to persuade him not to sit on my hand when he first got on board.'

'I'd better make sure he's in the other boat,' said Ivor. He cupped his hand to his mouth. 'Ahoy! Commander, me old sea dog!' The commander's boat was about 30 yards away and he raised a drunken arm in acknowledgement. 'Have you got Kelvin aboard?' There was a flurry of activity in the other vessel as they lifted cushions, peered into baskets and looked under the rowers' benches.

'No!' yelled back the commander. 'You've got him. I saw him trying to give Jimmy a kiss as he got on board.'

'I told you I thought I remembered him,' said Jimmy. 'But he sure as hell ain't here now. Poor Kelvin! He must have drownded.'

There was a moment's silence for Kelvin as we thought of the trout picking at his eyeballs.

'I wonder if Prudence will sell the farm,' mused Bill. 'I might be interested in making her a fair offer for it.'

'I should think she'd want to continue farming it herself,' said Jimmy. 'She's been doing all the work by herself for long enough.'

'That splash!' said Ivor. 'It can't have been a shark at all. It could have been Kelvin falling overboard. Let's go back and take a look.'

'There's no point in that,' replied Bill. 'He'd have gone to the bottom ages ago.'

'No, he wouldn't. It was only a couple of minutes ago.

Anyway, if they find they have lost a man overboard on one of the Atlantic liners, they about-face and go steaming back for hours to try and find him. And sometimes they do.'

'That's different,' said Bill. 'This isn't an Atlantic liner.'

'That's true,' acknowledged Ivor, 'but I think we ought to make some sort of an attempt to find him. If we pull him out, we've got Lindy on the other boat. She could probably resurrect him with mouth-to-mouth. So I suggest all the rowers turn round and start going back the way we came.'

With considerable trouble, the oarsmen about faced, rocking the boat dangerously as they did so, and went back the way they had come, trying to recall where they had zigged and where they had zagged. Bill was stationed at the stern, which were now the bows, to keep his eye on the water to watch for any Kelvin-like jetsam floating about.

'I think it would be a bit unfair to expect Lindy to do mouth-to-mouth on Kelvin,' said Bill, picking up the conversation where it had been left off.

'Why?' asked Jimmy. 'Nurses are trained for that sort of thing.'

'I know that,' replied Bill scornfully, 'but can you imagine doing it to Kelvin? Would *you* do it? Think of his false teeth, for a start. If he ever takes them out, I reckon he marinates them in horse piss. I can't think how else he'd manage to get them so yellow.'

'Aye,' said Jimmy, 'I can see what you mean.'

'Keep your eyes on the water, Bill,' said Ivor from the bows of the boat.

'Keep your hair on,' came back the reply. 'I am keeping my eyes on the water. . . . Speaking of hair, have you ever heard of scraggy grey water weed?'

'No,' said Jimmy.

'Half a mo, then.'

While the boat slewed to a halt as the oarsmen dug in their blades, Bill rolled up his sleeves and plunged his arm into the water by the side of the boat. He groped around for a few seconds, his eyes closed in concentration and then brought up his dripping hand. Clutched in it was some hair, attached to the end of which was Kelvin's face. As the face broke surface, the eyes opened with a manic glint in their depths. A fist erupted from the water to the left of the face and narrowly missed Bill's nose. 'Bloody hell!' exclaimed Bill, and smartly let go his grip. The head sank beneath the water again. 'Back off a bit,' he said, and the rowers dug in their oars and pulled the boat a bit further away. The head came up again.

'You bunch of bastards!' it yelled. 'Chuck me overboard and then leave me to drown. I'll teach you!' Kelvin started to thresh the water towards the boat.

Jimmy wailed in fear: 'Be careful! Don't upset the ship. I can't swim.'

'Back off a bit more,' said Bill. The oarsmen needed no encouragement.

'Hit him with an oar,' suggested Jimmy. 'He's in a drunken frenzy. It might quiet him down a bit.'

'I'll get you!' yelled Kelvin. 'I heard that. Trying to hit me with an oar!' He was building up quite a foaming bow wave in front of him.

'Be careful, Kelvin,' said Bill. 'Don't forget you can't swim.'

Kelvin stopped. A stricken look crossed his face. 'Christ! That's right, I can't swim!' He threw up his arms and disappeared beneath the water.

'Thank God for that,' said Jimmy, who was crouching in the bottom of the boat for safety. 'Let's go home.'

'We can't just leave him to drown,' objected Ivor as Kelvin's imploring eyes re-appeared above the surface and he opened his mouth. His words were lost to posterity as the water flowed in and he sank again.

'I don't see why not,' said Bill. 'It's not murder or anything. I'm sure just not rescuing somebody is not against the law.'

'Polluting the reservoir with dead bodies. That'll be against the law. And it's us that has to drink the water from it, remember.'

Kelvin didn't drown, of course. The commander found a rope at the bottom of his boat and threw it across to him, along with an inflatable bed on which Mary Mowbray had sunned herself during the afternoon. Kelvin was towed back, beached near the harbour and left to find his own way home once Lindy had established that alcohol was at the root of his problem rather than straightforward senile dementia. He turned up in the pub the following day and his behaviour of the previous afternoon was never mentioned by anyone again – except when he became drunk, abusive or irritating, which was no more than a couple of times a week.

Chapter Three

THOSE WHO live and work in a rural environment find it difficult to show much enthusiasm when a nature-loving townsman bounds into the pub bearing a wilting weed, even if it is worth innumerable points in his *I-Spy* book. To the discoverer it may be a rare and wondrous thing. But the farmer to whom he is talking has probably been trying to eradicate it from his cornfield for ten years and fails to be infected by the nature buff's excitement. In fact, most environmentalists tend to be as popular in the village pub as a Mormon missionary at a cardinal's conclave.

The resident nature bores in our locality were the communards who tried to practise self-sufficiency, with considerable help from the state, in a decaying country mansion with a few acres attached on the edge of the parish. They believed that anything invented in the past thirty years was a bad thing and that their hens should be allowed to roam free so that they were all eaten by foxes, and that machines and herbicides were anathema which meant that their scraggy crops were soon overwhelmed by nettles and fat-hen.

Only one communard ever made the difficult transition from being one of the weirdos whose doings were a source of amusement and entertainment, to becoming one of the real people in the rest of the parish. Dick had been one of the original members of the commune when it had been a post-Dylan colony of gently balding hippies, still hoping for the triumph of Peace and Love in the cruel world of the eighties. But gradually his contemporaries had fallen by the wayside. One started to sell life insurance; another was picked up in the

Channel sharing a yacht with a ton or two of cannabis with the inevitable consequences; while yet a further couple returned to Streatham, whence he travelled up to the West End every day where he worked as manager of an exclusive fashion salon.

Dick soldiered on, but his cracking point came when the new members of the commune decided to adopt ancestor worship as its established religion. Dick had been a devotee of many obscure gurus in his time but he came from three generations of Wolverhampton hairdressers and, while he was able to respect them, he found it impossible to make the quantum leap across into worshipping them. So Dick decided to leave the commune and rejoin the human race, albeit the rather obscure rootlet of it that flourished in the parish.

He found himself an empty farm cottage to rent and set himself up as a jobbing gardener to the old ex-colonial drunks who liked to look over their roses and delphiniums during warm afternoons when the ice was tinkling in their gin-and-tonics. He came to realize that the world of nature was not the Elysian Fields with man as the asp that spoils it, but a balance of terror with each fox needing 2000 vole-equivalents a year to keep alive. Life in the real countryside with people who had to earn their living from it did not destroy his faith in nature but it allowed him to observe it through the rather jaundiced eyes of the rest of the community.

Dick's knowledge of the wildlife of the area was phenomenal. There were one or two hiccups before he was able to change his beliefs, built up during his years in the commune. For instance, he put himself through considerable angst with some bracken. The farmer across whose hillside it had spread wished to spray it to allow grass to grow in its place to feed his sheep. That was just not on for a recently retired graduate of alternative environmentalism. Dick offered to cut it down instead, without charge (at this stage he still had the state's support), to show his dedication to the cause. The farmer was delighted to let him try. With sickle in hand, Dick worked his way steadily along the side of the hill in the summer sunshine and, by the time he had finished, the bracken was already a foot or more high where he had first cut. So he resigned and watched phlegmatically as the helicopter, hired by the farmer, clattered over and killed the lot in one spray-filled minute.

Dick, a small nut-brown man in his thirties, was always being stopped to be asked questions by tourists wanting to hear an authentic local accent. They would back away, appalled, from the sound of the Black Country that issued forth. It was an understandable mistake because Dick really looked the part of the traditional countryman. He always wore old brown moleskin trousers and brown boots with a spiral of First World War surplus puttees round them and his calves in wet weather. He scorned gumboots as nasty modern inventions. He wore a striped cotton shirt without a collar and braces holding up his trousers. He did not believe in feeling the cold and his only concession to winter was a sleeveless khaki pullover that he donned between November and March.

Dick was a natural person to turn to when the pub suffered its infestation. It started quietly enough. The hostelry was going through one of its more popular phases. The normal cycle of this estabishment was that it should be bought for about £70,000, be tarted up a bit and passed on a year later for £85,000, then get sold again a year or two later for something over £100,000, at which point the buyer would find that the custom attracted would not pay for his bank loans and he would become alcoholic and bankrupt in swift succession, after which the price would slump and the cycle would begin again. It had been recently bought by Helga who was about as different from the usual run of landlords as it was possible to get. She brought an unprecedented touch of glamour to the community. Nobody knew very much about her background or the source of her money and nobody wanted to inquire too closely. In a village where everyone knew everything about everyone else, this was extremely unusual. But Helga seemed to be a creature of exotic fantasy. People were afraid that she might disappear or turn to dust if they found out some mundane truth in her background. We wanted to believe in her like children believe in Tinkerbell.

Helga had the ability to make the most arrogant of the old chauvinists who were the patriarchs of the community roll over like puppies to have their bellies scratched whenever she lifted her finger, and there was great competition between them for her favours. They washed up glasses, manhandled barrels of beer and even chucked out drunks at her slightest whim.

On the day when the infestation started, most of the regulars were present. They were deep in conversation about the price of nitrogen fertilizers while a couple of the more powerful ladies of the parish, Lindy and Mary Mowbray, were discussing the local doctor's seat on a horse. It was a peaceful tourist-free time of the year, just before Easter when the hordes descended.

The locals always drank in the public bar, the lounge bar being exclusively reserved for tourists as a ghetto where they could do all the things they liked, such as playing loud music on the juke box, having sing-songs and wearing shorts and tight scarlet T-shirts so that they could show off their tans and bellies to each other. Normally this bar was closed in winter but Mandy and Keith, a couple of summer swallows that had decided to settle in the area, still retained their urban desire for exotic drinks like rum and passion fruit which could only be supplied from the multi-coloured shelves of the lounge. Keith was present that afternoon, telling the bar about his amazing new plastic honeysuckle that he had just tacked all over the front of his cottage. It had a lot going for it. It bloomed all the year round, did not attract insects and had a small receptacle at the bottom which contained an aerosol can of scent with which he sprayed it whenever he wished to sit out of doors. It even came with extensions so that it could appear to grow from year to year.

Keith wanted a whisky and blackcurrant juice, so Helga had to come out from behind the bar and go through into the lounge, switching on the lights as she went. She had been gone only a couple of minutes when she screamed.

'EEEE! Help! Help!'

There was a delay of a second or two before beer glasses

went flying as there was a concerted rush to reach the lounge first. The commander just led the field and was able to enfold Helga to his manly bosom, his sweater redolent of the horse manure that he had been spreading in order to promote the growth of his mushrooms. With his arms locking her so tightly that Helga appeared in some risk of suffocation, and the rest of the regulars spread in a protective phalanx round her, they looked for the reason for her screams. All appeared quite peaceful. There was a notable absence of rapists and there were no vampires lurking by the silent pinball machine.

'What's wrong?' asked Bill.

Helga pointed a trembling forefinger towards the regiments of fruit-juice bottles. 'There's a spider in there.'

'A spider?' Bill's voice dripped with scornful contempt before he recollected who had done the screaming. 'Oh, a spider! How dreadful for you!'

The commander clutched Helga closer. 'Don't worry, I'll sort it out for you.'

'No, I will,' said Bill. There was a run on the juice bottles as he, Kelvin and Keith all tried to outdo each other in a bit of dragon slaying. The commander was seriously tempted to join them but clearly decided that any kudos he gained from spider slaughter would have to be set against the surrender of his advantage in having current possession of Helga's person.

The others rapidly emptied the shelf of bottles and revealed the spider sitting rather self-consciously outside a small tangled web in the corner.

Keith gave a yell of triumph. 'There it is! Quick! Squash it!' He was hopping from foot to foot in his excitement.

Bill and Kelvin peered at the creature. As native-born countrymen, they always had a careful look before they leapt. 'You squash it, Keith,' said Bill.

'Me?' said Keith uncertainly, taking a closer look at the spider. 'I don't see why I should have to squash it. I found it, so somebody else can kill it. I don't like spiders anyway. I've never seen a spider like that. It's not like the ones I see in the bath. It might be poisonous or something.'

It was a rather unusual-looking spider, quite large as

spiders go, with a shiny black body about the size of a pea.

'Don't be silly,' said the commander confidently. 'You don't get poisonous spiders in this country. Someone get rid of the bloody thing.'

'Oh yes, please,' pleaded Helga. 'Bill, you're so brave. You do it.'

Bill shot her a thoughtful look before leaning forward to extend a horny thumb towards the spider. The creature allowed the thumb to come within about 6 inches of its person before it raised itself on half a dozen or so of its rearward legs and waved the remainder threateningly. Bill hurriedly drew back. 'Bloody hell! I don't fancy that. The bugger looks as though it's going to attack me.'

'Get out of the way, Bill,' ordered Kelvin. 'I'll sort it out.' He picked up a bottle of tomato juice and brought it sharply down on top of the spider. The spider exploded, along with the bottle, and the green gunge that spread out from its abdomen was swamped by a tidal wave of red. As the rest of them looked on in disgust at the mess, Helga unwound herself from the commander and gave Kelvin a smacking kiss. 'You were wonderful,' she said.

'I hope you're going to clear that up,' said the commander. 'It looks like the aftermath of a traffic accident.'

'Sorry about that,' replied Kelvin, blushing to the roots of his straggly grey hair as a result of the kiss. 'I didn't mean the bottle to break.'

'You should have used soda water. Then it wouldn't have mattered if it had broken,' said Bill. 'I hope you're going to pay for the tomato juice.' Both he and the commander were irritated that it had been Kelvin who had been the recipient of the kiss.

'I wouldn't dream of asking you,' said Helga. 'You were so brave.'

'Look!' exclaimed the commander, triumphantly wrapping his arms round the rather startled Helga once more. 'There's another of them by that bottle of whisky.'

This time the hunters had enough sense to grab a bar towel apiece as they moved into the fray, but much of the incentive had gone from the chase as the commander deemed it wise to remove Helga from the scene of danger so that she could pour him a barley wine in the bar next door.

After ten minutes of bangs, crashes and exclamations, the dishevelled butchers re-joined us. Kelvin and Bill had each accounted for another spider – Bill with his bare hand, which put him above his companion in the courageous spider-killing league – but they had to admit that several more had given them the slip under the bar counter and down a hole made by the pipes that led from the beer pumps into the cellar.

Helga was a full blown arachniphobe. She insisted that they seal up the lounge bar with strips of blanket and newspaper tacked round the doors, and she was adamant that nobody was going to be allowed down into the cellars until the spider infestation was over.

The following lunchtime, the expert arrived. Dick had been

sent for in order to give his considered verdict on the beasts and the best method of eradication. He would have been willing to come merely to satisfy his curiosity as to the species of spider, but he had also been promised a fee of a couple of pints of cloudy real ale, complete with bits and pieces in suspension.

Most of the regulars turned out to watch Dick at work. He parked his bicycle outside the pub and ducked in through the stone-lintelled door. The door provided one of the strongest indications of the hostelry's claim to be approaching a thousand years old. The building was thatched, but so were dozens of others. Its beams had ancient adze marks sculpted along their length, but they could be scarcely older than Tudor. However, the door was not only well under 6 feet high to give all the necessary access to the midgets who went before us, but the stone lintel had a perceptible hollow in it where centuries of skulls had made contact with shattering effect. Winnie, the professional village eccentric who had been burnt as a witch during one of her previous incarnations, used to clutch at her heart whenever she came through the door, complaining that the weight of people's pain down the centuries had created an atmospheric blackspot that was bound to affect the sensitive.

Dick was not sympathetic to the problem at hand. He made sure that he had his first pint in front of him before he allowed his opinion of the pusillanimity of the regulars to show. 'A plague of spiders! It's ridiculous. Spiders are lovely things to have around. They catch all the flies and their webs sift the dust out of the air. You should think yourself lucky to have them, rather than be frightened by them.'

'That's all very well to say, but Helga doesn't like them and I must say they're pretty nasty spiders,' said Bill.

'Don't be daft,' replied Dick. 'How can they possibly be nasty?'

'One of them threatened Bill,' said Keith.

'How?' demanded Dick.

'Well, it sort of waved its legs at him.'

'That doesn't sound like much of a threat. The Bluebell

Girls go in for leg waving and people don't rush to have them exterminated.' He took a long draught of his pint. 'I suppose I'd better go and have a look at them.'

The commander and Keith carefully removed the strips of carpet from the door to the lounge bar which held the spiders at bay. With Helga keeping well in the background, they went through into the darkened room which reeked powerfully and characteristically of stale beer and tobacco. Keith went over to the window and pulled back the curtains to allow the sun to flood in to the musty lounge. They looked about. There appeared to be a conspicuous lack of spiders.

'I don't seen any spiders,' said Dick. 'What did they look like?'

In the glare of full sun, it was difficult to imagine what all the fuss had been about. Bill, who had traded on his hero status as much as possible over the past twenty-four hours, looked a bit shame-faced. 'They were very unusual-looking spiders. Sort of black and shiny. Very ferocious-looking.'

'Black and shiny?' asked Dick.

'And green,' added Keith.

'They weren't green,' said Kelvin scornfully.

'Their insides were. Don't you remember?'

'I suppose they were. But the colour of their guts is no bloody use as a description.'

'I don't see why not.'

'Of course it isn't. If I was telling someone what you looked like, I'd say you were a bit short and had a scraggy black moustache. I wouldn't say that you had 30 feet of guts inside your belly and that they were purple or green or whatever colour they might be.'

'Is this one of them?' asked Ivór, who had not been part of the great killing the previous day. He was indicating a large plate hanging on the wall which portrayed, in relief, a bunch of jolly smock-clad rustics quaffing ale.

They all went over to see. 'That's one of the little buggers all right,' said Bill, moving in with his horny thumb to flatten it.

Dick caught hold of his arm. 'Don't be in such a hurry.

Let's have a look at it first.' He had his look. 'How absolutely fascinating.'

'What's so fascinating about it? It's just a spider,' said Bill.

'Do you know what kind of spider it is?' asked Dick.

'Not really. It's not a money spider. I know what they look like, or I did before I had to get reading glasses, but it's you that's supposed to be the spider expert.'

'I've never seen one quite like this before.' He called out through the door of the lounge. 'Helga, have you been importing anything from America recently?'

Helga stuck a wary head round the door. 'What sort of thing?' she asked suspciously.

'I don't know. Whatever one does import from America. Baseballs. Indian bonnets. Cadillacs. That sort of thing.'

'I can't think of anything. Why?'

'Because I think that's an American spider.'

'Don't be silly,' said Bill, scornfully. 'An American spider indeed! It took a package holiday into Heathrow, I suppose, and then came down here with a caravan.'

'It could have come over in something else. Odd insects are always turning up inside cargoes of bananas and things like that.'

'You don't see many ships unloading bananas outside this pub.'

'Well, I don't know how it got here, but I think it's a black widow. And they can be deadly.'

The commander was the first to react. He flashed between Dick and Kelvin and had Helga in his arms before she had time to gather her breath for the scream that set the tankards tinkling behind the bar and made the spider scurry for the protection of the web which it had built between the kneecaps of two of the ale quaffers.

Nobody else was hanging about either. The commander had to move Helga sharply aside to prevent her being trampled to death as Bill and Kelvin thundered through the door and out of the lounge. Keith chose a different method. He gave a squeak of dismay and scurried beneath one of the tables in the lounge.

The commander, trained to retain his control during emergencies, was first to gather his wits enough to speak. 'For heaven's sake, Dick, what are you talking about? Poisonous spiders, indeed!'

Dick strolled carefully through into the public bar. 'I may be wrong. But I've never seen a spider like that before and I saw a programme on BBC2 about black widows and it looks just like they did. Black and shiny. About the size of a pea. I think there's supposed to be a red hour-glass shape on their bellies as well. But I'm not sure.' He looked back over his shoulder. 'By the way, Keith, if you're trying to escape from spiders under there, you ought to know that they do prefer to hide in dark places.'

'What do you mean?' asked Keith, suspiciously poking his nose out from under the table.

'I mean that you're more likely to find a spider lurking under the table than you would be almost anywhere else in the room.'

Keith erupted from beneath the table like a Scottish lock forward who had just found the ball at his feet in the middle of the scrum under the English posts at Twickenham. In his enthusiasm he carried the table with him, but it was brushed off his shoulders by the frame of the door and fell violently to the ground, breaking into several pieces.

'You stupid berk!' said Ivor. 'Look what you've gone and done.'

'Sorry,' said Keith, moving towards the door of the pub. 'If you'll excuse me, I think I'll go and warn Mandy.'

'Warn her about what?'

'That there are poisonous spiders in the neighbourhood,' he said over his shoulder as he hurried through the front door.

'At least one good thing may come out of this,' commented Kelvin, 'if it drives that blasted Mandy out of the village.'

Mandy was one of the only people in the community who was scathingly rude to Kelvin to his face. The rest of us contented ourselves with being scathingly rude about him behind his back.

'About these spiders,' said Dick, and the rest of those present snapped back to attention. 'I am not absolutely certain that they are what I think they are, but I don't think we ought to take any risks, just in case.'

'Quite right, darling,' said Helga fervently.

Dick acknowledged her agreement with a courteous nod. 'I think that we ought to call in the council who are best equipped to deal with this sort of thing.'

'They may be quite good at cockroaches, but I doubt if they would have had very much experience of black widow spiders,' remarked the commander.

'You're quite right,' agreed Dick, 'but at least they're geared up to handle this sort of problem and they ought to have the experts on hand who could at least give us a certain identification. I mean, we may be panicking for nothing.'

'But that means bringing in Bert,' said Kelvin.

'That's right.'

'What's the point of that?'

'At least pests are his job.'

Bert was the council rat catcher and he had made the parish his own. It had taken him nearly a decade to get all the farmers and land owners round about to allow him on to their premises on search-and-destroy missions without any warning needing to be given. He hounded the local rats with gun, gas and poison. We were the testing ground where he tried out all the esoteric methods of slaughter that his rat-hating brain could dream up before unleashing them in the rest of the county. Kelvin had entered his barn a few months earlier and had touched a trip wire that had set off a flash camera in his face. It had nearly given him a heart attack and had not warmed him to Bert who had a theory that a species of monster rat lived in the chaos of Kelvin's farm which should be photographed before he committed genocide.

Dick was given the pub telephone to summon skilled aid while the others, under the direction of the commander and Helga, once more re-sealed the lounge bar before departing about their various businesses.

'I'd like to be put through to the pest officer, please,' Dick said, after explaining who he was and where he was calling from.

'I'm afraid he's out. Can I take a message?'

'Yes, I'd be grateful if he could come out as soon as possible.'

'What'y'got then? Rats? Killer bees?'

'No, spiders.'

'Spiders! Is that all? You can't have Bert out for spiders. Spiders aren't pests. All you have to do is put a glass over the top of them and slip a bit of cardboard underneath and then empty them out of doors.'

'They're not ordinary spiders. I've never seen any quite like them before. I think they're poisonous.'

'Poisonous! Coo! They're not those great big hairy ones like you get in the horror movies?'

'No. They're the sneaky little black jobs.'

'Like the ones you get in your bath? They're not poisonous. Anyway, you don't get poisonous spiders down here. Bert's never been called out to poisonous spiders before.'

'Well, he has been now.'

'Oh, all right. I'll pass the message on to him. Spiders, indeed!'

The evening's drinking session was a subdued affair. Kelvin was there, wearing gumboots with his trousers tucked inside to make sure that no spiders should crawl up his trouser leg and bite him. There was even a sprinkling of irregulars: people like Malcolm Jarrett who taught in an education college 20 miles away.

Word of the black widows had got out and fear stalked the deserted streets to an extent not seen since a rather nosy tourist, who had gone round most of the village shops, had been suspected of being a VAT inspector. There was a bit of desultory talk about the falling price of calves and the harvest prospects and a little speculation on whether Michael Green and Mary Webber might be having an affair and whether or not their respective spouses knew about it. Kelvin, self-styled village godfather, brought up the subject on everyone's mind. He had obviously been doing some thinking.

'What are we going to do about these here bugs? That's what I'd like to know.'

'I think we can safely leave it to the ratman, tomorrow, Kelvin,' replied the commander.

'I don't think that's good enough. All our loved ones are at risk. Quite apart from ourselves. Think what would happen if one of those beasts came in here and started biting.'

'The dog it was that died,' murmured Malcolm Jarrett.

'What's that?' asked Kelvin sharply.

'Just a line from Goldsmith,' replied Malcolm.

Kelvin had a profound contempt for anything he could not taste, touch, see or spend and education came high on his list of life's unnecessary fripperies, so he ignored the interruption and continued, 'I think we ought to take precautions.'

'What sort of precautions?' asked the commander.

'This is an emergency, so I think it's only right that we should activate the emergency committee.'

'That's a dreadful idea,' said Dennis hurriedly. Dennis described himself as a gentleman farmer, which meant that he did as little work as possible, keeping only a few bullocks, and drank an enormous quantity of whisky, for the supply of which he relied on his wife's substantial private income.

'Why?' asked Kelvin. 'It's an emergency, isn't it?'

'Yes, but it's not the sort of emergency that the emergency committee was trained to handle.'

This was a very sensitive area. The committee had originally been set up to protect the village in the event of nuclear attack. It had become apparent during a series of exercises, when annoying little men from County Hall had tried to tell the doughty volunteers what to do, that there was no possible way to protect the village in the event of nuclear attack and that the emergency volunteer system was just an excuse for a lot of grown men to play boy scouts. The committee had resigned *en masse* and had allowed Kelvin, a Cromwell guiltless of his country's blood if ever there was one, to take the whole thing over and ask some of his more Neanderthal cronies to join him. Dennis had suggested that they should change the name of the organization to the Klan and that Kelvin should be called the Grand Dragon, which had quite appealed to him, but headquarters had refused to agree to it.

Kelvin's strategy in the event of war was to impound all the foodstuff in the community and lock it up in the church hall while he stood guard with a shotgun to shoot anyone who tried to take anything. This had led to a secret meeting of the parish council and the appointment of Gerald Mowbray, a farmer of stout thews and a direct if simple mind, to shoot Kelvin as soon as the Russians dropped the bomb to prevent him doing any damage.

'The emergency volunteers are trained for anything,' said Kelvin. He looked round the pub for some of his lieutenants, but there were none present.

'You would need to get the approval of the parish council

before the volunteers could be activated,' said Ivor.

'Not necessarily. In the event of breakdown of the normal democratic process, I am empowered to take over.' Kelvin's desire to wield power was greater than that of any politician and he saw potential emergencies everywhere.

'I'm sure that's true,' agreed the commander, 'but I don't think that the democratic process is in danger of breaking down just at the moment. After all, there is quite a difference between a large quantity of megatons being dropped on our heads and a few spiders wandering about in the lounge bar.'

'It's just a matter of degree,' argued Kelvin. 'Nobody could deny that poisonous insects could constitute an emergency.'

'That's a big word, Kelvin,' remarked Lindy. 'And spiders aren't insects.'

'Constitute? It means—'

'Isn't that a spider on your leg, Kelvin?' interrupted Ivor.

It wasn't. It was only a speck of cow dung. But it was enough to drive all thoughts of power from Kelvin's skull and send him hurriedly out of the pub as soon as he had finished his pint and established that there was nobody else who looked willing to buy him another.

The jungle drums in the village muttered and grumbled all night and a great killing took place. By morning the streets were littered with the corpses of a great multitude of spiders, slaughtered in a great pogrom by the fear-driven populace. The Great Spirit above took note of the event and sullen clouds built up above the village and the sky wept.

Bert came splashing into the village in his minivan at about noon the following day and went straight to the pub where he was met by Dick and the rest of the curious. Helga had left the premises at closing time to move in with a neighbour and was not going to return until the all-clear had been given.

Bert was a familiar figure in the parish owing to the frequency of his ratting excursions. He was about forty and astonishingly good-looking with dark Latin-lover features which attracted most of the damsels on the farms into darkened hay barns to hold his poison for him. He only scored with real country girls who had sufficiently strong and experienced stomachs to cope with the miasma of sewers that impregnated his person and his van, thanks to the many subterranean expeditions he undertook in pursuit of his normal quarry.

Bert entered the pub, the dull thud of his skull on the lintel bringing a certain phlegmatic satisfaction to those present. He spent a couple of minutes on his knees, moaning and rubbing his head before he recovered sufficiently to come over to the bar. He looked at Dick in surprise. 'You're not involved in this business, are you?'

'Yes.'

'Poisonous spiders? I was sure that it must have been some daft old biddy who'd found one in her bath. You're not serious are you?'

'Go and have a look.'

'Look where?' he asked, peering round the bar.

'Oh, sorry. They're in the lounge. It's all sealed up to stop them spreading.'

'I see. Well, they're not going to be going anywhere very far. I might as well have a drink first, now I'm here.' He looked hopefully round the others present, but nobody volunteered to put their hands in their pockets. 'Kelvin?'

'I don't mind if I do,' said Kelvin. 'I'll have a pint.'

Bert looked outraged. 'I'm hoping *you're* going to buy *me* a pint, not the other way round. I've got rid of enough of your rats for you.'

'Sorry,' said Kelvin. 'I don't believe in buying drinks for other people. I'm a Methodist.'

'I heard you use cigarette papers instead of lavatory paper, Kelvin,' said Dick.

There were snorts of laughter from the others while Kelvin's face assumed a glazed look as he tried to work that out. 'What do you mean by that?'

' "Mean" is right,' replied Bert.

'Why don't you look at the spiders first and I'll buy you a drink afterwards,' offered Dick.

Bert looked a bit sulky, but he had no alternative unless he was prepared to buy his own beer. Dick carefully removed the towels and wads of newspaper that had been re-stuffed into the cracks round the lounge door and Bert entered and looked round, observed from the doorway by the locals clutching their pints protectively to their bosoms.

There was one of the spiders sitting in the corner of the bar. It must have been a busy night as there was a thick tangled web to its rear. Bert looked at it ruminatively.

'Now there's a thing,' he said, still thoughtfully rubbing his skull. 'It's a funny-looking little beggar, isn't it?' he continued, turning to Dick who had been the only person brave enough to enter with him into the bar. 'Have you seen one like him before?'

'Only on television.'

'Yes. I heard that it was supposed to be a black widow, but I thought it was just blethers. I mean, I'm always being called out to do something about funny-looking ladybirds because people think they're Colorado beetles. But, you know, I'm not so sure about this.' Bert went over to the work surface and peered down at the spider. 'I ain't seen anything quite like this before. Nasty-looking little bugger, isn't it?' He poked at it with his forefinger and the spider obligingly went through its leg-waving act for him. 'That's called a threat display,' said Bert knowledgeably. 'Aren't many spiders that put on a threat display like that.'

'Why don't you get on with it?' said the commander. Bert was leaning forward and gently blowing at the spider which was working itself into a bit of a temper, judging by the rapid series of press-ups which was its reaction to the breeze. Bert paused and looked round. 'What do you mean, "get on with it"?'

The commander was a bit taken aback. 'You are the exterminator aren't you?'

'That's right,' agreed Bert. The spider took the opportunity of the sudden drop in wind speed to scuttle into its web for shelter.

'Well, exterminate then. Spray the room or whatever, and kill everything in it,' said the commander.

Bert sucked in his breath. 'Can't do that, I'm afraid.'

'Why the hell not? That's what we got you out here for and it is your job, isn't it?'

'That's my job, all right. But I can't go around killing things that are unknown. It could be anything, this beast. A species new to science, in which case it would certainly be protected by law; or, if it's been imported from somewhere else, we have to find the source and make sure that no more come in, particularly if it's a poisonous spider. And I have to admit that it looks a bit suspicious. Anyway, I think I've seen enough here. Dick, I'm about ready for that drink, now.'

Bert returned to the public bar and watched while Dick poured him a pint. The voyeurs clustered round, waiting to find out what he was going to do next. He knocked back a large draught of beer and smacked his lips appreciatively. 'Pity about the weather, isn't it?' he said conversationally.

'Yes. But what are you going to do about the spiders?' asked the commander.

'The spiders? I suppose I ought to get on the telephone and find someone who might know something about them.'

The commander leant over the bar, pulled up the telephone and plumped it down in front of Bert. 'There you are!'

'Let me finish my beer first.'

'Make the phone call, then finish your beer. The sooner these damn insects are out of here, the sooner we can all get back to normal.'

'There ain't no need to worry about a few spiders.'

'Kelvin's gone around telling the village that we've got a plague of black widows. And everyone's in a bit of a flap.'

'Oh. If Kelvin's going round stirring things up, then it does make a bit of a difference.'

'Damn right it does.'

Bert picked up the telephone while the rest of us re-sealed the lounge door.

'It's all sorted out,' he said a few minutes later. 'The Ministry of Agriculture are sending out a couple of entomologists. I told them that I agreed with Dick and that they were probably black widows and they said that they'd be out within a couple of hours. Who's going to buy me another pint?'

The emergency, together with the absence of Helga, provided an opportunity to ignore the normal licensing hours. Percy, our local policeman, looked in and seized the chance to extract drinks from everyone in return for not enforcing the law. The Dunkirk spirit was abroad in the pub although everyone made sure that they stayed down the far end of the bar away from the door to the lounge. A beer barrel ran dry while they waited and Bert, with Dick covering his back with an aerosol can of insecticide, bravely went down into the cellar to change it.

By the time the experts arrived, the gathering had developed into a really good crisis party. The man in charge was pointed towards the spider still sitting peacefully on the

plateful of rustics and he whipped out a little net and neatly popped the creature inside a jar. He was not messing about. He came back into the bar. 'Telephone!' he snapped. It was provided. He dialled through to headquarters. 'It's a black widow all right. I've got a sample and I suggest that we send it up to the Natural History Museum for a definite confirmation. Meanwhile we'll get on with clearing the area.'

It was quite a hairy business. A team descended on the village and pumped noxious chemicals throughout the pub and down into the sewers and made careful inspections of most of the houses round about. More spiders were found in the house immediately next door and the extermination teams moved in, spraying and gassing as they went, in spite of the protests of the elderly occupant who claimed she had never been afraid of spiders in her life and saw no reason to start being afraid of this one. Matters were beginning to look quite

nasty and there was some talk of putting the village under a movement restriction order to prevent the spiders taking over the country.

Then word came back from London. They were not black widows. They were not even poisonous. They belonged, in fact, to a rather obscure species of cave spider that was normally to be found in Cornwall. Although they were not actually protected by law, added the letter, they were extremely interesting and completely harmless and the fact that they had extended their range so far from their original habitat was ecologically fascinating and an arachnicologist would be coming down to investigate the following week. Even Helga agreed that it was a pity they were all dead.

Chapter Four

THE PRECISION of the social hierarchy of the countryside broke down with the Second World War. Before then, everyone knew exactly where they stood, to whom they could be rude and to whom they must tug their forelocks. The squire was at the top of the social tree. Then followed the vicars, rollicking hunting Philistines throughout the nineteenth century, who had left their work to be done by the pale and trembling curates, at least one of whom, legend has it, was defrocked after being found *in flagrante* with a nanny goat. They represented the gentry, and beneath them was the doctor, then the larger farmers, the tradesmen who did not dirty their hands, the tradesmen who did and, finally, the peasants.

That was then. Now the squire was just a farmer like any other. The vicarage had been bought by an antique dealer and the minister of the few souls that were still interested in being ministered to whizzed through the village on Sunday morning in his Fiesta, tossing wafers and communion wine out of the window as he hurried to cover the five churches in five parishes that were his responsibility. The doctor had his practice based a dozen miles away; the skilled tradesmen were down to a few scrub mechanics, the myriad of different shopkeepers were reduced to a handful and only the farmers still soldiered on in the same sort of numbers that had been there before. Even the pub had lost the eight rivals which had formerly competed to satisfy the bucolic thirsts of the village's ancestors.

We had gained one professional – the vet. Our vet was a brave man. The United Kingdom consists of a network of jealously guarded territories. It is not only the birds and animals who fight to maintain their own exclusive patches over which they hunt to feed their young; people do it as well. The solicitors, estate agents and builders mixed happily with each other, sharing the same territory just as robins, blackbirds and tits can share the same garden. However, should another of the same species or profession intrude, then they bristled, fluffed out their feathers at each other and did their best to drive out their rivals, determined to protect their own interests and food supply against those of their opposing colleagues.

Our village and its surrounding farms were part of the veterinary territory of a group practice of half a dozen partners who covered a large chunk of the country. The vets were computerized and hammered round the countryside between calls in a fleet of fast saloons. The senior partner even managed to pass off a light aeroplane as a legitimate business expense, although the only time he had tried to land it in the parish it had caused a herd of cows to stampede into the river. The local livestock was used to the thunderous jets of the RAF skimming down the river, sometimes dropping their under-

carriages in an alarming game of chicken to see if they could touch the water without coming to grief. But when the senior partner decided to visit an urgent calving in response to this buzzer going off in his pocket during an afternoon's spin and came over the trees sounding like a demented chainsaw to land in a field next to the river, the cows rebelled. Their life was supposed to consist of peaceful dreams amid the buttercups while they made milk. A foot- or wheel-borne vet was bad enough. He always seemed either to stick his arm up into their innards in a gross violation of their bodily integrity or else stab them with needles and force a variety of noisome liquids into them. When the bastard turned up like a fixed-wing angel of mercy, it was definitely time to go and jump in the river.

Bernard Bessington-Omerod was a most unusual vet. He first turned up in the area attached to the established practice as a student in search of experience. He was an exception to their normal rule of only taking on females for the practical part of their course. It pleased all the partners to speed round the countryside with pretty young girls by their sides, and it pleased the local garages as their cars were often hitting hedgerows in mid-grope. Bernard was male, if a little precious, and extremely well-bred, having gone to a good school and being rumoured to have titled ancestors. He would have fitted in beautifully to the budgie-and-borzoi belt in SW3 where the rich dowagers would have adored his vague, little-boy charm, but out in the sharp end of the business we were used to a stouter breed of vet: those who could wrestle a yearling bullock into submission whilst holding a syringe in their teeth, or could plunge an arm to shoulder-depth up the arse-hole of a bull to stimulate it to ejaculation, ignoring the terrible tourniquet effect of the mightly bovine sphincter. (Cattle have to have powerful sphincters as efficient as those of the whale: the latter has to keep *out* liquid under pressure, while the average cow has to contain a seething cauldron of substances resembling the aftermath of a vindaloo curry consumed at a backstreet stall in Bombay.)

Bernard was a breath of fresh air in the neighbourhood. As

a student, he was not expected to be much of a vet. Few farmers require much of the vet anyway. They know their stock and the ailments to which they are subject as well as any professional, but they need the vet to get access to bottles of antibiotics to pump into them. Therefore Bernard's incompetence did not really matter and he did brighten up normally dull days. He was asked to examine rams that were having difficulty in lambing, milk bulls and inject bunches of young pigs that had been carefully greased beforehand. He could have had a laugh every hour of the day or else beaten the brains out of his tormentors. But he neither laughed nor wept; he just plodded on, accepting the practical jokes with a rather worried expression on his appropriately chinless face and falling, delightfully, into every trap that was set for him. When he went back to university, the farmers were all rather sad to see him go.

Then a brigadier's widow died in her house near the pub. Within a month its cellar containing 3000 empty gin bottles had been cleared and the house bought by Bernard, who stuck a brass plate on the door announcing that B. Bessington-Omerod, MRCVS, was open for business. It was courage beyond the call of duty to trespass so openly on the territory of such a powerful bunch of professionals as the local vets and they soon began a campaign to drive him out. They went round their customers casting aspersions on his competence. He would have been asked to join them, they said, after he had graduated had he not been so piss useless. The farmers found many of the vets that they sent round piss useless already, so that charge carried little weight. They even put pressure on the drug dealers. Anyone who supplied Bernard would lose their business. That did not work very well either, since there were plenty of shady characters who could supply anything from the boot of their car from streptomycin to sten guns and so he did not go short of the necessary equipment.

Bernard found that a substantial proportion of the local farmers were prepared to give him a try. It was nothing to do with the charm of his baby-blue eyes, but a matter of hard finance. The other vets with their virtual monopoly were ruthless in collecting unpaid bills, sending out their Sierra-driving commandoes on the first day of the month to dun any of their clients who were late in paying. This was deeply resented. Ordinary businessmen do not like paying bills and farmers are extraordinarily tight-fisted businessmen, particularly where the vet is concerned. Vet bills were traditionally paid, partially paid at least, once a year after harvest or after the sale of the year's crop of lambs. If prices were poor, the vet was lucky if they settled at all.

Bernard either understood this system or was too well-bred or chicken-hearted to go and ask farmers for money. It was not long before the group vets discovered that they had lost their really bad payers and the unprofitable tail end of their list and so they began to warm to the existence of Bernard. Our parish contained a high proportion of poor payers – farmers who saw no reason why they should pay a vet's bill unless the patient fully recovered – but Frank Mattock, who considered himself to be a bit of an agricultural whizz kid, was mortified when the aviating senior partner suggested that he might consider switching his allegiance to Bernard. The fact that he had owed £1000 for eighteen months was no reason to remove him from their list.

Bernard had private means, otherwise he would have starved, but even so he was awarded the almost unique privilege of being allowed tick in the pub which was right next door to the house he had bought. Helga's tender heart had ached for him when he staggered in at opening time, hair awry, chinless chin trembling with emotion and eyes filled with horror at the dreadful veterinary experiences he had had to undergo in the agricultural underworld that was now his sphere of operation. He fell in at the deep end on his first day, being summoned to visit a difficult calving by Gilbert Clattermole.

Gilbert Clattermole was one of the old school. In our part of the country, that meant a very old school indeed. He was a true peasant, about forty-five, going bald, illiterate, dirty, social-security numberless and unknown to the Inland

Revenue. It was believed that a tax inspector had unearthed the fact of his existence about a decade earlier and had gone to visit him. At the end of the afternoon, the inspector had left, but not before he had torn up Gilbert's newly created file to ensure that no other member of the Revenue should ever have to meet him again. One of the lesser difficulties that the inspector would have encountered was that Gilbert believed in neither bank accounts nor record keeping. In fact, it was doubtful if more than a couple of hundred pounds went through his hands in any given year, since almost all his dealings with outsiders were done by barter.

Gilbert called up Bernard on his newly installed telephone. (He had it for two months until British Telecom took it away again when they realized that Gilbert was under the impression that telephone calls were free once the device was in place.) 'It's Bessie,' he had announced. 'She's calving and I can't sweeten it out.' There were many strange ways of persuading cows to yield up their calves. Frank's favourite method was to affix a rope from the calf to his tractor tow bar and pull. That was the juggernaut school of calving which could result in bits of the calf or the cow becoming detached from the main body with consequent deleterious effects. Gilbert believed in the efficacy of placing a heaped teaspoon of demerara or white sugar by the cow's vulva. This was supposed to be irresistibly attractive to the calf, which would fight to get clear of its mother, while the type of sugar determined its sex: white for a bull and brown for a heifer.

It had been very exciting for Bernard: his first client/patient on his first day. He had donned his green surgeon's outfit, just like they wore in hospitals in American TV serials, which was unused and pristine, as were his instruments and his bottles of antibiotics – a virgin vet without a splatter of dung anywhere on his person. It was unfortunate that Gilbert was the first customer. It should have been someone like Frank Mattock where he would have visited his patient in the immaculate holding pen off the milking parlour which Frank scoured down with a pressure hose twice a day after each milking and then sprayed with disinfectant. If one did not mind the risk of carbolic poisoning, one could eat one's dinner off the pen floor. Certainly no bacteria could survive.

It wasn't like that at Gilbert's, however. Had he ever given the matter any thought, he would have been of the opinion that if God had meant stock to be free of germs, he would have blessed them with a disinfectant gland to add measured doses to their dung. Gilbert's farmyard had not been mucked out for years. Due to the scarcity of livestock on his farm – he didn't want money, so there was no reason to give himself work – the couple of feet of dung that raised the ground level of his yard above that of the surrounding countryside, had decayed to a pleasantly friable and sweet-smelling humus, but the number of tiny little beasties that lived and copulated there would have led to a prosecution being taken out against him by the RSPCA, had an Inspector ever stuck a dung fork into it.

Bernard drove down the lane, biting his lip in anxiety as the bottom of his new car crunched on the ground while it dipped and swayed its way through the potholes that were home for some storm-tossed tadpoles. He parked in front of the house and Gilbert came out to greet him, pulling his braces up over his shoulders as he passed through the door. The curtains of the Clattermole living room were always drawn, for he and his wife began watching television at 11am after he had done his morning chores and stayed in front of it until the national anthem came on around midnight. His wife was almost unknown locally since she rarely visited the village. On the rare occasions that she came out of their house, she looked like some nervous cave animal as her eyes blinked suspiciously at the hard bright world that existed beyond the safe insulation of her living-room curtains.

Gilbert led the way across his farmyard towards a dark stable doorway, framed by nettles which thrived on the rich compost in which they were rooted. It lay in the centre of a long barn, half of which had been the original farmhouse before Gilbert's father had put up the current prefabricated dwelling before the war. Now the loft of the barn and the first floor of the house had been knocked through to store hay and straw and the two small rooms in which generations of little

Clattermoles had been reared were homes for chickens and calves. The calving cow was in the original barn and Bernard had to adjust his eyes to the darkness of the interior before following Gilbert's tracks up the mountain of ancient dung that filled it to waist height, in order to reach the cow.

She was tethered in one of the old milking stalls with her head held down so that it nearly touched the ground. The chain was cemented into the wall at the correct height but the dung had built up so much that it was now barely a foot off the surface. The first thing that Bernard did was to untie her so that she could stand up properly. He looked worriedly at her back end. She had the swollen vulva of a calving cow, but there was no evidence of an offspring and only the scattering of white sugar to show that she had been straining. She was a beef animal – a Hereford/Friesian cross – so Gilbert wanted a bull.

'Er,' said Bernard, as the cow rolled her eyes at him while he rustled and crackled in his new green waterproof gown, 'would you please get me a bucket of warm water and some soap, please?'

'She wants a calf, not a bath,' said Gilbert.

'It's for me. I want to wash my arm before I introduce it and the soap acts as a lubricant.'

Grumbling, Gilbert went off on his errand while Bernard and his first patient continued to eye each other uncertainly. It would have been difficult to decide which of them was the more nervous about the coming encounter; in fact it was probably Bernard, for his patient was a Clattermole cow and Clattermole stock had to be very near death before Gilbert called in veterinary help. They saw vets so rarely that they did not associate strangers in funny clothes with the outrages that make vets so unpopular amongst all right-thinking livestock.

Bernard stuck his arm up the back end of the cow to sort out the tangle of limbs inside and began to pull. The cow had obviously been straining for some time and so Bernard needed to apply a lot of soap to lubricate the calf's passage to the outside world. He also had to tie ropes to the animal's legs, once they had emerged, to give him a better pull. Throwing his soul into the business, he looped the rope round his back to give himself greater leverage and, as Gilbert looked gravely on, the cow ran around the pen a couple of times, bouncing Bernard through the dung behind her. It was very old dung, so Bernard did not suffer unduly and, after picking himself up, he eventually managed to extract the calf. He was administering some brisk slaps to its flank to clear mucus from its lungs and encourage it to breathe when Gilbert spoke.

'Well done. That's not a bad calf. If it's all right by you, there's another thing I'd like you to take a look at.'

'I'd be delighted to,' replied Bernard, on his knees by the calf. 'What is it?'

He looked over his shoulder and was extremely alarmed to see Gilbert taking his braces off his shoulders and pulling down his trousers. Apart from his lack of chin, Bernard was a good-looking young man, in an inbred sort of way, but he had not been given the wind up like this since he had been approached by a prefect in a school lavatory when he was fifteen. As Gilbert began to pull down his incongruous underpants – cotton with pictures of Mickey Mouse on them – Bernard checked to ensure that his all-enveloping green suit was still securely fastened at the back and tried to decide how best to deal with the situation. Gilbert was his first and, so far, only client so he had to tread cautiously. He backed carefully to the wall, leaving the calf to the rough tongue of its mother.

'Mr Clattermole, I'm very sorry, but I don't do that sort of thing.'

Gilbert paused with his pants halfway down towards the top of his dung-encrusted bedroom slippers and his trousers.

'Course you do. You're a vet, aren't you? The last vet seemed to thoroughly enjoy himself. He said it was a pleasure to do it with a man rather than with animals.' Gilbert finished removing Mickey Mouse from the area of his loins and turned to display his ample and hairy backside to Bernard.

Bernard felt his forehead break out into a thin film of sweat. He had known that the countryside had been likely to be rather raunchier than his protected upbringing had prepared him for, in spite of five years at Eton, but this experience made

it look as though it could plumb depths beyond his most gruesome imaginings.

'What would your wife think, Mr Clattermole?' asked Bernard wildly.

'My wife? It was her idea to ask the vet in the first place. She thought it was silly to travel 20 miles for it when I was paying for him to come out already.' Gilbert looked sourly over his shoulder at Bernard. 'I suppose you can add it to your bill but the last vet said it was a pleasure.'

First customer or not, Bernard could feel himself beginning to lose his cool. 'Mr Clattermole, I really must insist that you pull up your trousers. For heaven's sake, we're in a cowshed!'

'That's what's worrying you, is it? We can go into the house. Do it in the bedroom if you like.'

'Mr Clattermole!' exclaimed Bernard weakly. Perhaps Belgravia would have been a better idea.

'I've been sitting in a bucket of cold tea for a week and that helped a bit,' continued Gilbert.

This *non sequitur* registered on the periphery of Bernard's brain as it was thrashing around feverishly for a diplomatic way out of the situation. Perhaps he could throw himself on the calf and pretend it was dying? It might distract its owner. Already Bernard knew that the prospect of losing money was the average farmer's deepest concern – next to the chance of making money. 'Tea?' said his tongue, puzzled.

'Like bunches of grapes,' droned Gilbert.

'Bunches of grapes?' What possible further horrors were about to be asked of him? He began to edge towards the door, pausing only to pick up his bag of instruments. He had left his calving cords tied to the infant's front legs, but Gilbert was between him and the calf. Gilbert suddenly noticed that he was trying to sidle away.

'Where do you think you're going?' he demanded.

'I've got another call to make,' replied Bernard, clutching his instruments to his bosom.

'But what about my piles?'

'Your piles? What are you talking about?'

'Yes, my bloody piles! What do you think I was talking about?'

'Piles!' shouted Bernard, a great wave of relief washing over him. 'You've got haemorrhoids!'

'Of course I've got bloody piles. What do you think I pulled my trousers down for? You're a vet. You should be able to do something for them.' Gilbert came out of his worries for long enough to register Bernard's relief. 'What's up with you? You look as though you've just heard that your mother-in-law isn't coming to stay after all.'

'Nothing, nothing at all,' replied Bernard innocently.

'About my piles, then,' continued Gilbert.

'I'm sorry,' broke in Bernard. 'Unlike your last vet, I know nothing whatsoever about piles. If I were you, I'd go and see your doctor, or keep sitting in cold tea.'

'You really think it does any good?'

'It can't do much harm as long as you don't drink it and, if you'll excuse me, I have another call to make. And if I give you any further advice, I'm afraid I shall have to add it to your bill.'

'That doesn't matter,' came the reply. 'I never pay the vet's bill anyway.'

It was not surprising that Bernard felt rather jaundiced with the world at the end of his first day and, by the end of his second, he had stopped asking for half-pints of shandy at the pub and was grimly knocking back the barley wines. By the end of his first week the worm had turned, and when he came into the pub at lunchtime on Saturday he was still spluttering with indignation.

He had received a telephone call at 3am from the Loosemires. Every community has its problem family and ours was the Loosemires. Bernard was too new an arrival in the village to have known about them. Father Loosemire was the postman and village peeping Tom. Nobody worried too much about him as he liked to peep only at Mrs Shapcott, who found it rather flattering. He had been peeping at her for decades and the longer it went on the more flattered she became. Even Mr Shapcott was rather touched when he still kept coming every Friday night after Mrs Shapcott had passed the twin milestones of sixty years and 16 stone. The loser in the deal was Mrs Loosemire who had to accommodate her husband when he returned from his Friday nocturnal excursions in a lather of lust, babbling about mountains of yielding flesh the colour of a 5p stamp. As a result there was a whole litter of little Loosemires, though now not so little, growing up surly, uncommunicative and wont to do the rounds of the neighbouring village discos on a Friday evening, looking for youths from the neighbouring towns with whom they would pick fights.

The Loosemires' phone call to Bernard had been to report

the state of their cat. It had been Jason Loosemire, nineteen and recently out of borstal, who had rung.

'Here, are you the vet? Took your bloody time in answering, didn't you?'

'It is three in the morning,' replied Bernard.

'So what? I've got an emergency. You must come out right away.'

'Yes,' replied Bernard, wondering, through his haze of sleep, whether he dare charge double time. 'What's the problem?'

'It's our cat. Its back legs have gone stiff.'

'At 3am?' queried Bernard.

'Yes. What's the time got to do with it?' asked Loosemire belligerently.

'Well, it's just that stiff legs are probably due to something like a touch of rheumatism and are not likely to constitute an emergency.'

'We think it's an emergency and the cat sure as hell thinks it's an emergency. It doesn't seem to be able to walk.'

'It would be a lot cheaper for you if you just put it in its basket for the night and brought it round here in the morning.'

'I'm telling you, it's an emergency. I think you ought to come out right away.'

Bernard sighed. 'All right. Where do you live?'

They lived about 2 miles out of the village, and Bernard grimly fought to extract comprehensible directions involving winding lanes and signposts that had been obscured by ivy. He then dressed, took his car out of the garage and set off. He didn't have much difficulty in finding his destination. In the countryside, life tends to shut down well before midnight and a house with lights blazing out across the fields could only have been the one he was looking for, although he made several abortive forays off the main road before he discovered that the lane that took him to it started off in the wrong direction.

When he finally drew up outside the house, he saw that most of the windows were open. Loud rock music was blaring out into the night. Still feeling rather dopey with sleep, he got out of his car and knocked at the door. He knocked for about five minutes until he was forced to pick up a stone and batter on the wooden panel; judging by the dents in the door and the white paint adhering to his selected rock, he had not been the first to use it for the purpose. The door opened. The opener, a man in his early twenties, was clearly drunk and had an aggressively punk female hanging on his arm.. The effect of her appearance, however, was softened by her eyes which were country-placid rather than street-wise.

'Yeah?' said the man.

'Er. . . Jason Loosemire?' asked Bernard.

'Who wants to know?'

'I do,' replied Bernard.

'I know that. But who the hell are you? You're not the fuzz, are you?' He looked at Bernard. 'No, you're not the fuzz. The fuzz don't look like you.' His girlfriend broke into giggles.

'I'm not the fuzz. I'm the vet. Mr Loosemire telephoned me about a cat.'

'Did he now? Hang on a second. I'll go and get him.' He turned from the door and disappeared down the passage towards the source of the rock music, leaving his girlfriend vacantly surveying Bernard, her mouth rhythmically chewing gum.

'Stop leering at the poor bugger, Bernadette,' ordered a slightly younger though just as drunk version of the first man, pushing the punk back from the doorway. 'Took your bloody time about coming out, didn't you?' he said to Bernard.

'You only called me fifteen minutes ago.'

'Fifteen minutes! I told you it was a bloody emergency. It doesn't take you fifteen minutes to come a couple of miles.'

'It does if you start counting when you're still in your pyjamas in bed. May I see the patient? Then I can go home again.'

'Sure. Come in.' Bernard allowed himself to be led through to the kitchen. The house was a typical 1930s barrack-style council house built in the days when the authorities had begun to accept the need to supply public housing for the poor but saw no reason why it should be either comfortable or well designed. It had been a Loosemire home since it had been put up and the council had long given up replacing plaster that had been kicked off walls or ceilings when feet had poked through them while stolen goods were being hidden. It was, therefore, a peculiarly charmless dwelling. In each of the four corners of the room blared an enormous speaker, and the water in the plastic bowl in which Father Loosemire was bathing his feet was trembling as the sound vibration rocked the house to its foundations.

Bernard smiled weakly at Father Loosemire. He recognized him as the deliverer of letters, although he was rather surprised to see him up. Postmen, in his experience, had to go to bed early as they had to get up early.

'Where's the cat?' he bellowed at Jason.

Jason cupped his hand to his ear and shook his head.

Bernard raised his voice to a maniacal scream: 'Where's the cat?'

This time Jason did not even appear to notice that he was talking as he had gone over to a cupboard and was pouring himself out a glass of beer.

Bernard felt his temper begin to fray at the edges. He moved over to the machine that squatted at the centre of its web of speakers and pressed a button. There was instant and total silence.

'Thank Christ for that!' said Father Loosemire.

'What the hell do you think you're doing?' demanded Jason, turning from his cupboard. 'I was enjoying that.'

'Where's the cat?' repeated Bernard.

'Over by the sink,' replied Jason, as he moved towards the record player.

'And keep that bloody noise off until I've examined it,' continued Bernard. 'How the hell am I expected to hear anything through my stethoscope? The cat's probably had its auditory centres destroyed and may well be suffering from further brain damage.'

He moved towards the sink. The cat, a rather moth-eaten tabby, was lying on the draining board. Bernard found that he did not need to utilize his many years of expensive training in order to make a diagnosis, nor did he need to use his stethoscope. The cat was dead.

'Is this the cat?' he asked.

'That's right,' replied Jason. 'Its back legs have gone all stiff and I don't think it looks at all well.'

'It's suffering from rigor mortis.'

'Is that serious?' asked Jason. Much as on the occasion a few days earlier when he had been trapped in the barn with an apparently sex-crazed Clattermole, Bernard was torn between laughter and tears. His ability to make up his mind which of the two paths to follow was not rendered any easier by the fact that it was 3am and he wanted his bed.

'You could say that it was serious. It only occurs several hours after death.'

'Is it suffering?'

'I said it's dead,' replied Bernard shortly.

'Dead? You mean you can't cure it?'

'The last living creature to be cured in the same condition as that cat was Lazarus. That was 2000 years ago and it was a miracle.'

'It wasn't dead when I telephoned you.'

'I'm afraid it must have been.'

'It was not. If you had come a bit quicker, it would have been all right.'

Bernard felt like bursting into the famous Monty Python sketch, substituting 'cat' for 'parrot': it's dead, deceased, a late cat, gone across the great divide, paid its penny to Charon, been harvested by the grim reaper. 'Your cat is as dead as a doornail. All its nine lives were used up by, I would think, about 8pm this evening.'

'Oh. What did it die of?'

'If you want me to find that out, I would need to do a post mortem which would not affect my prognosis on the animal one whit and would cost you more money.'

'More money! What do you mean "more money"? You're not going to try to charge for doing nothing at all?'

Bernard began to experience a buzzing in his ears the like of which he had not felt since taking part in a boxing match at school. His opponent had struck him on his nose and had subsequently regretted his temerity when Bernard had waded in and half-murdered him in his ensuing rage.

'Look, Mr Loosemire. You have called me out in the middle of the night to make use of my professional services. The fact that my diagnosis could have been given by a bloody moron, provided he had not been drunk, does not alter those facts and my bill will be fully in accord with the time of day and the circumstances.'

Bernadette had slunk into the room to find out why the music had stopped and was listening casually to the altercation from her position leaning against the doorpost. Jason appealed to her.

'Here, listen to that. He's saying that I'm drunk!'

'Well you are, aren't you?' answered Bernadette unhelpfully. 'Drunk as a skunk. Gary said that the bleeding animal was dead, but you still had to go and phone for the vet.'

'I wasn't sure, was I? I didn't think it looked dead. Just a bit stiff.'

'You're a right bloody berk, Jason Loosemire.'

'So I was wrong. But he's got no right to go and send me a bill for doing nothing.'

'Yeah. That does seem a bit stiff.'

'Yeah. Look, mate – '

'I am not your mate,' said Bernard. 'My name is Bessington-Omerod.'

'You poor old bleeder. I bet your first name is Cecil,' said Bernadette.

'No, actually. It's Bernard,' said Bernard.

'Look, Bernie,' said Jason, 'why not just have a little drink and we'll forget about the bill?'

Bernard would not be moved. There was a principle at stake. His other clients watched with gradually increasing respect as he doggedly fought for his bill to be paid over the ensuing weeks. It went through two reminders, a solicitor's letter, a summons and a county court judgment which joined the sheaf of other writs outstanding against the Loosemires.

The conclusion was a tit-for-tat when Gary Loosemire thoughtlessly did some work on Bernard's car and was told to whistle for his money. Although Gary was the wrong Loosemire, the considered opinion of the village was that justice had been done. Some of Bernard's other customers were sufficiently impressed to start paying their bills. In spite of his effete exterior, he had shown himself to be a vet who was not to be trifled with. Not too much, anyway.

Chapter Five

IN SPITE of the desires of ninety per cent of those who lived in and around the village, all sorts of things seemed to conspire to make it a tourist attraction. To most of the inhabitants, tourists were nothing more than a nuisance. Their coaches, caravans, cars and bodies clogged everything up and slowed everything down when their swarming season came round. The cafe, those who took in bed and breakfasters and the various shops found profit in them, but they were very much in the minority.

On sunny summer days, the village could have been posing for its calendar photograph. There was the vivid green backdrop behind the houses of the tree-covered hillsides. There were the neat thatched houses with their colourful cottage gardens. There was the river, its clear bubbling water spanned by its medieval bridge, and, right at the top of the village, there was the church with its humped graveyard that was a mass of crocuses and daffodils in spring. All that lifted the community from this ghastly cliché of English country life was its people. They did not go round in smocks, chewing grass and knuckling their foreheads at the sophisticated urbanites who came out to visit, but ripped them off, or tried to run them down in their cars and managed to behave towards them as if they were members of a lower race of mankind – which, of course, they were. By definition a tourist both exploits the places that he visits and is exploited by them.

Over the years, villagers had been doing what they could to discourage the tourists by uglifying the community. Many of the thatched cottages had been re-roofed. Those that had been

bought by the affluent retired had been covered in slate or tiles, while those who still needed to earn the meagre country living on the farms and in the shops put on corrugated iron which soon turned red with rust under the ceaseless showers that came down from the moorland above us. There had even been a rash of modern bungalows erected on the approaches to the bridge in an attempt to de-prettify the village, but nothing worked. Nature still conspired to make the area beautiful, in spite of the best endeavours of the populace.

One example of the uncaring way that Nature treated the wishes of the villagers was to be found in the ducks that lived on the river. They had a fluctuating population but, over the course of the year, there averaged about thirty individual birds which lived on the 200-yard stretch of the river as it ran through the village. They were a horrible, mongrel crew consisting of a basis of mallard with dashes of Indian Runner, Khaki Campbell and Aylesbury thrown in. These birds had evolved purely in response to the tourists. In the same way that various birds and animals are supposed to be able to foretell the hardness of the winter or the fineness of the summer by their behaviour, so could these ducks foretell the number of tourists that were going to be coming for the season. The first clutches of eggs would hatch just before the Easter weekend when the visitors would first arrive, and the number of ducklings that wandered about was always shrewdly matched to the quantity of feed that the tourists would supply.

If these creatures had stayed on the river or on its banks and waited for the tourists to come to them, they would have been less obtrusive. But they did not. They harried visitors like the child beggars of Calcutta, demanding crumbs, cakes and sandwiches while the visitors, not realizing the ruthless way in which they were being exploited, found them sweet and stuffed their greedy beaks with goodies.

It was painfully obvious to the beholder that the ducks looked on their young only as useful accessories in their search for food, for the lack of maternal care shown to the offspring was lamentable. Ducks would sneak up to each other's broods and drown them if they should appear to attract more food than their own; drakes would kill their young when they encountered them; and there was a fatal flaw in the use of the leat above the weir as a ducks' nursery. It was fairly fast-flowing and had several waterfalls upon it where the old mill wheels used to be. Any unwary duckling that allowed itself to be distracted by a piece of succulent bread or weed from the task of paddling continuously, in order to keep its place in the family convoy, would find itself swept away over the mill races and totally unable to re-make contact with its siblings. Such refugees ended up eventually in the main river where they would wander round for an hour or two or three, peeping piteously, before falling prey to a passing drake, heron or crow, or else be swept way down the river to the badlands to the east, from where no riverbound traveller returned.

Reluctantly, but inevitably, the villagers found themselves drawn into the fate of these ducklings. Most people were connected with farming or actually were farmers; the one cardinal agricultural crime is waste and these ducklings represented waste in its most heinous form. Potential meals – crisp sizzling skin, tender breast marinated with orange – were, for the want of a month or two's basic care, being squandered on the broad, uncaring face of the river. Then there was another reason for the locals' interest which was never admitted to: there can be nothing in nature, except possibly a young koala bear, that is so skilfully designed to appeal to the tender recesses of the human heart as a duckling. Writers from Beatrix Potter to Hans Christian Andersen have known and exploited this fact. At the beginning of the duckling season, one would see hard-bitten characters like Bill or Kelvin leaning over the edge of the wall that bordered the leat, looking down with concern at some separated youngster and, if they thought that nobody was looking, they would bend down and sweep it into captivity in their cap. They would then croon at the fluffy little bundle of yellow or speckled feathers – the colour dependent on the degree of miscegenation that its parents had been up to – with its tiny duckling beak that opened to peep trustingly up at its captor and saviour.

There was always the problem of what to do with the ducklings once they had been rescued, as it was often impossible to identify the particular family from which they had come. One year, Dick announced that he wanted as many ducklings as possible. He had moved from the commune into an ex-gamekeeper's cottage on the top of a hill just outside the village and was hard at work turning himself into a real countryman, earning his living from a bit of contracting round the local farms, a bit of tree felling and a bit of poaching as well as his gardening.

Dick was building himself up some kind of a smallholding in his back garden. He had a few hens wandering about, some goats which he used to milk and a young red deer hind which he had rescued when its mother had been shot on a poaching escapade. It was a fairly silly collection of creatures with a whiff of the commune about it, but Dick was a recognized local eccentric and he could be forgiven his aberrations.

The back garden of the pub tended to be the local collection point for rescued ducklings and, when a few had been gathered in, they were taken up to Dick's house or else he came down to pick them up. One Saturday, when the current number of refugees had built up to six, Helga and Lindy decided to take them up to Dick during the course of the afternoon, as much to have a look at Dick's house as to get rid of the ducklings.

Dick lived in a tiny example of stockbroker Tudor at the end of a rough track in the midst of a conifer forest. He rented it from a local farmer, but rarely had to pay. Many of the farmer's previous tenants had been the hard country boyos who could become extremely violent when they had taken drink and Dick, as gentle as a lamb, profited by this. His landlord had once tried to put up the rent of a previous tenant at 10pm one Saturday evening and the response had given him such a fright that he rarely could screw up his courage to go to collect his money when it was due. Dick did not mind. He pottered happily about his tiny estate and probably never even noticed that his rent was months behind. He was out the back of his house, fiddling with his bicycle, when the ladies arrived with their goodies.

Dick thanked Lindy and Helga prettily for the ducks and asked them in for a cup of tea – an invitation that was accepted with alacrity, since entry into his house was the main purpose of the expedition. The interior of the house was a reflection of the man. It fitted Dick like a well-worn overcoat. A few female refugees from the commune, their minds destroyed by irrational philosophies and drugs, would come and live with him for a week or a month, but they never stayed long enough to make any impression upon its contrived disorder before drifting off again to seek some purpose to their dreary lives. The kitchen was piled high with dirty crocks, sprinkled with a scattering of pheasant feathers – although the opening of the shooting season was still some months away.

Dick ushered them into his sitting room. It had a brown carpet and a small wood-burning stove in the fireplace. There was a bookcase containing volumes on birds, beasts and flowers, while the wall creaked under the weight of a couple of dozen sets of antlers which tended to be the local symbol of virility. People scoured the moors during spring in search of cast antlers and, together with those given out by the hunt for services rendered, they were highly prized possessions to be mounted and preserved or traded and sold for surprisingly large sums of money. There were skins of foxes, deer and goats scattered over the floor and the chairs, and in one window sat a stuffed tawny owl. It was a horribly masculine establishment and the women perched uneasily in their seats to the accompaniment of sounds of shifting crockery from the kitchen as Dick sifted through the debris for a supply of cups.

'Do you think it was a good idea that we stayed?' whispered Lindy from a sofa placed in front of the window. 'Judging by the mess, we may pick up some nasty disease.' As a nurse, Lindy was particularly conscious of such things.

'I should think it would be all right, although I had expected that Dick's house would be filled with Buddhas rather than dead animals,' replied Helga.

'We'll probably pick up fleas at least,' continued Lindy gloomily. Dick had a large black, flea-ridden Alsatian that he kept chained up outside when he was present and released when he went out so that it could guard his property. It was a locally notorious animal since, if you visited his house, it would come bounding over and jump on you. If you were not ready for it, or were not strongly built, it would knock you off your feet and proceed to do its best to kill you through drowning you with huge slaps of its great pink tongue.

Dick came bustling back through, bearing three large mugs of brown liquid. 'I assumed you all take sugar,' he said cheerfully.

'Sometimes,' replied Lindy, as she took one of the mugs and

gave it a cautious sip. 'I do quite like tea with my sugar, though.'

'It'll give you extra energy,' replied Dick.

There was a short pause while Helga and Lindy wondered what to say next. Dick was a silent man by nature and neither Helga nor Lindy were used to social gatherings without small talk.

'It's a very interesting room,' said Helga politely. 'You've got some fine sets of antlers.' Helga could not have cared less about antlers, but as landlady of the pub she had learned something of her customers' interests.

'Are you interested in deer?' asked Dick.

'Well, yes,' replied Helga cautiously.

'I've got a little present for you, then,' said Dick.

'A present? Oh, how very sweet of you.' Helga had probably, since puberty, been the recipient of presents from men with whom she was barely acquainted and she had learned to accept them gracefully as her due. Dick went to a drawer and removed a small furry object and passed it over.

'Dick! You didn't buy that at the knickerware party did you?' asked Lindy.

'Certainly not,' he replied as he handed it over. 'I made it myself. It's a purse.'

'How nice!' said Helga, turning it over and putting her hand inside. 'Thank you very much. You made it from the skin of a deer? It's beautifully soft inside. It's absolutely lovely, isn't it, Lindy?'

Lindy took it from her and stroked it. 'There doesn't seem to be a seam. How did you stick it together?'

'I didn't need to. It's a purse.'

'Yes, I know that. You said so already, but what part of the deer is it made from?'

'A purse. A stag's purse. Its scrotum.'

Lindy knew what a scrotum was and delicately placed the object on the arm of her chair before changing the subject.

'What exactly are you going to do with the ducks? You're not going to rear them to sell their eggs are you? Duck eggs can be very dangerous if the birds do not live in scrupulously clean conditions. Salmonella, you know. I might have something to say about it if you tried to do it from here.'

'Don't you worry. I'm not going to be selling any eggs.'

'Good.'

Helga suddenly let out a little scream. 'Your owl! It blinked!'

Lindy turned to the window where the bird was sitting on a branch about 18 inches away from her. 'Don't be silly. It's stuffed.' The owl suddenly opened its beak and clicked it several times. 'Good heavens! It's alive!' She hastily moved to the other end of the sofa, away from the bird. 'What the hell's a thing like that doing here?'

'That's Twit,' said Dick proudly. 'He's a owl.'

'Yes, I can see that,' replied Lindy testily.

'I've had him for coming up for a year now. He's very affectionate.' Dick moved his hand towards the owl and started to stroke its breast feathers. The owl clicked several more times, fluffed up its feathers and sank its beak into Dick's finger. Dick gave it a buffet with his free hand and the owl hissed at him. 'Bastard thing,' he said, sucking his finger. 'It must be hungry.'

Lindy withdrew to another chair, out of range of the clicking beak and away from the purse. 'Where did you get it?'

'I was chopping down a tree last season and there was a nest in it. One of the chicks was killed straight away and Twit had a broken wing. It's mended now but he doesn't seem too keen on flying away. I climbed up a tree with him the other day and dropped him, but he just fell to the ground like a dead chicken. He's been in a bad mood ever since.'

'Poor little thing,' cooed Helga, which earned her a look as poisonous as only an owl could deliver and another ill-tempered bout of beak clicking. 'Is little diddums hungry?'

'What do you feed it on?' asked Lindy. 'I don't suppose a packet of birdseed would get you very far.'

'No. Owls eat meat. I used to get a supply of dead day-old pheasant chicks from the rearer down the road, but his birds have got beyond that stage now, so I have to scrabble around a bit. But those ducklings you brought up will do very nicely.'

Helga looked horrified. 'You can't mean that you intend to feed those dear little babies to that foul creature, do you?'

'Of course. That's what I want them for. They're just about the perfect size. I'll show you.' Dick left for the kitchen and returned with the pathetic remains of a duckling. 'Incidentally, I don't need them to be alive like the lot you just brought. Twit prefers them to have been dead for a day or two so that they're getting nice and gamy, and I can always stick them in the deep freeze. So I don't mind if you bring them up dead.'

Before the horrified eyes of the two women, he tossed the duckling to Twit who deftly fielded it and made a gallant attempt to swallow it whole. He got stuck just before he completed his meal, which left him with a couple of small web-footed legs sticking out on either side of his beak. For some reason it looked quite extraordinarily obscene.

Lindy was appalled. 'I think that's one of the most revolting sights I've ever seen.'

Even Dick seemed rather shaken by the macabre spectacle. 'He normally manages it in one gulp,' he said. 'It was quite a large duckling,' he added apologetically, clicking his fingers at Twit who managed another gulp which left merely the feet dangling out. It did not really improve the way he looked. 'I think it's time we were going,' said Lindy, rising to her feet.

'Yes,' agreed Helga. 'How many ducklings has your owl eaten?'

'Dunno, really. Must be about thirty, I suppose. You've been bringing them up quite regularly over the past few weeks.'

'About those ducklings we just brought in. Do you think we could have them back?' said Lindy.

'What for?'

'Well, I thought I might rear them,' said Lindy.

'What did you bring them up here for, then?'

'We didn't know you were feeding them to that bird. If we'd known that, they might as well have stayed in the river and died there.'

'But Twit's putting them to good use.'

'I'm sure he is, but it's not quite what we thought was happening to them.'

'If that's what you want,' said Dick, who obviously failed to understand what the fuss was about. They went outside to the shed where he had put the ducklings when Lindy and Helga arrived. The door of the shed was open and there were no ducklings to be seen – only a rather guilty-looking black Alsatian at the limit of its chain, thumping its tail ingratiatingly as they approached.

'Bad dog,' said Dick unconvincingly. 'It looks as though we're too late.'

'So I see,' said Lindy. There was a certain frost in the air as they said their goodbyes.

Kelvin, Bill and all the others who spent their time rescuing ducklings did not quite know how to react to the information that the women had uncovered. They were all hard-nosed countrymen who took a certain pride in the ruthless way in which they sent much-loved cows for slaughter or sent a shiver of horror up the spine of any visiting tourist when they despatched a chicken with a casual and much-practised flick of the wrist. Dick was behaving absolutely in the true rural tradition and yet, like any lily-livered townsman, they found the idea of their carefully harvested ducklings being fed to an owl extremely difficult to cope with.

There was a debate in progress in the pub as to what the foundlings' future should be, when Ivor came in. He had been fishing in the river downstream of the village and, as well as a selection of tiny trout, he had caught a duckling. It was pounced on by the newly established protectionists of this species who had thrown all dignity and caution to the winds. Kelvin and Bill broke into gruesome baby talk when he dumped it on the bar.

' 'Oo's a dear little ducky-wucky, then?' crooned Kelvin as he leant over the unfortunate bird which took one look at his bristly grey whiskers and blackened, ill-fitting false teeth, gave a squeak of terror and dived off the edge of the bar. Kelvin tried to catch it in a palm so calloused that a cut had to be half an inch deep before it would draw blood, and, instead of duck, caught hold of a strand of fishing line which left the bird dangling upside down by its legs. 'What's this, then?' he demanded accusingly, as he held it up for all to see.

'Put the poor little bugger down, Kelvin,' ordered Bill and the duckling was deposited back on the bar where it lay on its back and looked sorry for itself.

'I told you I caught it when I was out fishing,' said Ivor apologetically. 'I made a cast and this creature just swam straight into my line and got itself in a most frightful tangle. I did not catch it with the hook so it ought to be all right.'

The duckling was spread out over the bar while a circle of faces peered down at it.

'He's a bit funny-looking,' said Bill. 'I don't think he's very well. He's big, mind you.'

The various bastardized genes that filled the cells of our duck population seemed to have come together to produce a rather odd little specimen. It was yellow below and mottled above and looked a bit larger than most.

Jimmy leaned over to have a look. He was a little bit blind and his vision was further obscured by the rolling bank of smoke issuing from the cigarette that was always stuck to his bottom lip. The duckling coughed as his miasma swept over it. 'I think he might turn out to be one of those Russian jobs.'

'A muscovy?' said Kelvin. There was some dismay in his voice. We had one pair of them on the river and they were the least popular individuals among the duck population. They showed even less respect for human kind than the other ducks and, being twice the size of the mallards, produced turds of twice the dimensions, twice the slipperiness, twice the odour and, it appeared, at twice the frequency. 'Ah well, I don't suppose any of us can help who our parents are. Helga! Have you got a pair of scissors?'

With Bill and Ivor helping to hold the patient still, Kelvin, breathing heavily through his mouth, began to snip away the fishing line which swathed the duckling. His first snip removed a patch of down about the size of a ha'penny and his second neatly cut off one of the bird's toenails.

'For heaven's sake! How many pints have you drunk?' asked Bill, as the next snip nearly removed his finger. 'You're going to chop the little bugger in half next.'

'It's not that I've been drinking, it's just that I haven't got my specs on,' said Kelvin.

'Well, put them on then, you silly old fool.'

'I haven't got them with me.' Since Kelvin could barely read anything except the fatstock prices which only appeared in his paper once a week, he rarely bothered to carry his glasses round with him.

'How about looking through a glass of beer? It should work as a magnifier,' suggested the commander.

'Not in this pub, it won't,' retorted Bill. 'I haven't been

served a clear pint of beer for the last three landlords.'

The duck seemed to have understood the threat that it was under as it began to struggle in a rather hopeless fashion.

'Shall we give it a bit of brandy to calm it down?' asked Bill.

'No, just hold it tight.' Bill and Dennis each had hold of a wing, while Ivor and the commander held on to the legs. By more luck than judgement, Kelvin managed to snip through a vital strand on the fishing line and the duckling's bonds fell away. The liberator sat proudly back. 'There!'

'What are we going to do with it now?' asked Bill.

'Isn't it sweet?' said Helga. 'Let's call it Donald.'

'Why don't you raise it here?' suggested Ivor.

'Here?' said Helga.

'Yes. Once it grew up, you could always eat it, I suppose.'

'That's what I'd suggest,' said the commander. 'If you were too squeamish yourself, you could always serve it in the restaurant.' The pub had long had the custom of selling deep-frozen, microwaved rubbish to tourists who were not capable of recognizing or appreciating good food, but Helga was doubtful.

'We never do duck,' she said. 'Chicken in the basket is very popular and scampi, but I don't think there would be much of a demand for duck.'

Bill and Kelvin had been listening with growing discomfort.

'You couldn't eat this little duckie,' said Bill. 'We've just saved its life.'

'Don't worry. Nobody's going to eat this little duckie. We're going to wait until it's a big duckie,' replied the commander cruelly. He stroked the head of the duck. 'Isn't that right, little fellow?'

'Peep,' said the duck, as it closed its eyes appreciatively.

'There's no room for sentiment when it comes to rearing livestock,' continued the commander, pompously parroting the lectures he had been given when he first came into the community. 'Life in the countryside is a hard taskmaster for man and beast alike and each depends on and exploits the other.'

'That's quite true,' said Kelvin. 'But you can't really mean that you'd eat this little chap.'

'Just watch me,' replied the commander, cheerfully. 'However, if you were to buy me a few drinks, I would consider changing my mind.' He did not need to consider it.

The duck was installed in the garden behind the pub and fed on rejected scampi and anything else that it could scavenge. It was given the free run of the pub, spending much of its time sitting in the bread oven to the side of the huge open fireplace, demanding crisps from the customers, and it began to grow.

It kept on growing until it turned out not to be a duck at all, but a goose, a Canada goose. By the time it was half-grown, it was testing the limits of its power. The other web-footed denizens of the locality would beg for hand-outs from the tourists. The goose would wake in the morning, decide what it wanted to eat for breakfast and then go for a gentle constitutional round the village. If it found a tourist or even a local eating anything, it would waddle up for a look and, if it approved, it would grab it. If one dared to object, the creature would raise itself to its full height, hiss and flap its wings and, if the objection continued to be made, it would start pecking.

It behaved equally badly in the pub. It shat on the floor, which was not quite so appalling as it sounds since the carpet in the public bar was encrusted with the offerings of generations of agricultural gumboots; a little extra from the bowels of the goose was neither here nor there. But it also shat on the bar and sometimes even on the pub cat.

Sentimentality was all very well, but there were limits to what the pub's customers would tolerate and Donald, as this brute was firmly labelled, would have speedily been despatched to join its ancestors because of its revolting behaviour had it not had one supreme cardinal virtue. It did not seem to like anyone very much: it attacked dogs, children, women, cows, cars and ducks with complete impartiality, but what saved it was that it was always willing to drop whatever it was doing to assault Kelvin. It grew up to hate Kelvin with a deep implacable loathing. This was not apparent during the creature's goslinghood, when Kelvin would scoop the bird up from whichever corner of the pub in which it was trying to hide and carry it over to the bar to scratch and tickle it with a finger that must have felt like a dibble, all the while uttering a tuneless, mindless crooning. Initially the bird was too small to make any objections to this, but as it grew it began to peck at his finger with all the understandable malice that it could muster and this Kelvin interpreted as a sign of spirit. As it continued to grow, it would run at Kelvin, hissing and flapping its wings, which Kelvin managed to decide were signs of affection.

Even this manifestation of extreme shrewdness when it came to character judgement was insufficient to maintain Donald's reputation. His popularity rapidly drained away when he began to assault and beat up the local dogs which most people were more attached to than their children. He even had the temerity to brave the wrath of Mandy by visiting the garden of her gnome-ridden cottage to uproot all the plastic flowers, shit on the shubunkin in her tiny pool and upturn a pot of pink paint, with which she had been touching up the window frames, all over the patio. A petition was raised to propose the bird's liquidation and even Kelvin was moved to consider it when it came across his van parked in the street and proceeded to rip off its windscreen wipers and defecate copiously all over the bonnet. Percy swore that it had nearly taken off his hand when he had tried to interrupt this act of wanton vandalism and he pored over the books that he had once studied, in a vain attempt to pass his sergeant's exam, to find out whether a goose could be charged with assaulting a police officer in the course of his duty. Part of the trouble was that Donald was owned by nobody which meant that nobody took responsibility for his behaviour or could be sued for any damage that he caused.

Then Donald became a hero. One bright and sunny afternoon he was sitting outside the butcher's shop begging for bits of offal and bones which the butcher, showing an appropriate sense of humour, tried to ensure came from ducks if he could not find a goose, when three small boys on bicycles

came along the street past the post office. There were plenty of witnesses around to see what happened next. One of the reasons that Donald found this a satisfactory vantage point was that it commanded a right-angled corner, which meant that Kelvin could be seen well in advance from whichever direction he approached and an attack could be prepared. The streets were narrow at this point – in fact they were narrow everywhere – and lined with thatched cottages and multi-coloured tourists meandering slowly between the church and the bridge which crossed the river at the bottom of the village.

The small boys were locals and, like all the locals, cousins, uncles, nephews of each other, products of the incestuous pavan that had whiled away the pre-television evenings for several centuries. Donald unfolded himself from the butcher's doorstep as they swooped down the road towards him, much faster than was safe under the circumstances. He waited until they were 20 yards from the corner before making his move. He launched himself into the air with a mighty hiss and flap of wings, and crunched into the leading cyclist just as he came to the junction. The impact knocked the boy off his bike, bringing down the second rider while the third just managed to stop.

As Donald grabbed his victim by the throat with his beak and began to disembowel him with his scrabbling feet, the second part of the drama had got under way. The village had no mains gas and so a large lorry turned up once a week loaded with three layers of gas cylinders to power the heaters and cookers of all those who were rich enough to afford to buy and use them. Victor was unloading them and Victor was not the smartest person in the community. He decided that it would be easier to unload the cylinders from the bottom with the obvious result – obvious to everyone but himself – that the greater part of the load was deprived of support and came cascading into the road making a noise like every cutlery factory in nineteenth-century Sheffield being picked up and shaken at the same time. If the small boys had been still astride their mounts and travelling, they would have been pulped. As it was, only Donald was in the way, gallantly shielding the body of the boy with his own. Donald was missed by the big cylinders that looked like blue dustbins, but was caught amidships by a small one. He was not a quitter. With the dreadful cacophany of a hundred cyiinders cascading all over the road, bringing the dead snorting out of their coffins in the churchyard under the impression that the Lord had decided on a last timpano instead of a trump. Donald, one wing trailing in the gutter, turned on the offending cylinder and proceeded to give it a drubbing. Victory his, he fainted gracefully on the pavement.

It was generally agreed that Donald had saved the life of the three boys. He hadn't been trying to beat them up. He had been trying to interpose his body between them and disaster. It was an example of selfless courage that was rare in humans, let alone in geese. He was a hero and carried his broken wing, which had been plastered by Bernard, proudly round the village, beating up cats, assaulting old ladies and generally behaving like his old self.

It was very sad when the commander ran him down in his car, just a day or two after Donald had broken into his rabbit house and caused around twenty of his does to die of heart failure. A terrible tragedy, it was, and the local paper gave him an obituary. Kelvin wanted Percy to prosecute the commander for dangerous driving, but it was not to be. Donald is still with us, stuffed, above the fireplace in the pub. Dick did the stuffing, and even if Donald's neck does sag a bit and even if he was extremely smelly for a couple of months, everyone agrees that he's much nicer how he is than how he was. Even Kelvin has come round to it at last: he gives him a stroke whenever he goes into the bar and Donald doesn't seem to mind a bit.

Chapter Six

THE COMMANDER was not a practical man. What skills he possessed were cerebral rather than manual. He could play a reasonable game of chess, had once completed the *Daily Telegraph* crossword on the day of publication and could say 'good morning' in at least a hundred languages, almost emptying the pub when he had proved it. However, when it came actually to turning theory into practice, he was not so good, which made it all the more unfortunate that he should have chosen to supplement his pension during his retirement by running a market garden.

He had tried other things as well. He had bred quail, but a fox had got in and killed them all. He had tried chinchillas, but had found them so pretty that they had ended up in the house as pets instead of being turned into fur coats. He had even tried to sell life insurance and had been so impressed by his training that he had bought enormous policies for himself and his wife but had subsequently resigned when he discovered that his earnings, gleaned from the cynical farmers who had cut their teeth on their first insurance salesman when the commander had been still doing PT at Dartmouth, amounted to rather less than the premium that he had to pay for his own policies. He was currently into rabbits and was discovering that their enthusiasm for premature death would put a lemming to shame.

His wife, Elfrieda, was the daughter of an admiral. She would never have claimed to be all that smart. The traditional admiral's daughter is supposed to single out the brightest young officers to whom to hitch her wagon. But Elfrieda had taken on the commander who had grimly struggled up the promotional ladder until he finally became irretrievably stuck when he had driven his boat into an American merchantman. Elfrieda looked a bit like a friendly camel and usually wore an air of pained resignation when she went to chivy her husband out of the pub at closing time, or to placate the greengrocer who had found rather more slug than lettuce when he had bought from her the meagre surplus left by the pigeons and the commander's own marauding pigs. Local opinion had long respected Elfrieda as a good worker, but she had never made much of an impact on the community – not until her husband made an unexpected impact on her.

It all began when the commander found himself a gatepost. He had strung up an electric fence to keep his bald Jersey cow, his pigs and his two sheep apart from his cabbages and had then found he needed a gate so that he could wheel his barrows between the two enclosures without being bitten by the fence. He had discovered the iron axle of an old farm wagon in a hedge and decided to use it as a gatepost. It was about 8 feet long and 3 inches in diameter and was a splendid lane-combing, even if there was the probability that it would short out his entire system.

George Loosemire, father of the afore-mentioned delinquent family, was the village's informant on the circumstances of Elfrieda's metamorphosis. He had been passing in his post office van and had stopped to watch the episode. Elfrieda had been detailed to prop up the post while the commander stood on a step ladder and prepared to wield the first mighty blow that would drive it a couple of yards into the soil. He raised the hammer, his moustache glinting as its nicotine-stained white hairs caught the sun, and then swept it down with the grace of a fishmonger splashing down a large cod on a slab. The hammer caught the top of the post a glancing blow and continued down to strike Elfrieda on the back of her head. She let go the post and sank to her knees. The post sagged against the steps and brought them and the commander down into some redcurrant bushes. George had been entranced. He had left his van and come into the cabbage patch so that he would

miss nothing. It was quite a few seconds before the commander had recovered sufficiently to begin to splutter.

'You clumsy idiot! Why let the thing go? If you had to let it go, you might have made sure that it was going to fall the other way. You might have killed me!'

As he slowly extricated himself from the bush, the commander became aware that answer came there none. Elfrieda was sitting back on her heels with a silly expression on her face clutching the back of her head. The commander clicked his tongue in annoyance. 'Come on, old girl. I hardly touched you.' He picked up the mallet and wiped the head absently with his hand. There was blood on it. He started. 'Good grief! I say, are you all right?'

She wasn't. George volunteered his van and they whipped her off to the local doctor where they were shown straight into the surgery.

'Hmm. Whatever happened to you?' asked the doctor. Elfrieda was still wearing her fixed and stupid expression and the commander had to answer for her.

'We were putting in a gatepost and my sledgehammer slipped.'

'Hmm. Nasty crack it must have been. Broke the skin. I don't think there's a fracture, but I would recommend taking her to the hospital for an X-ray to make sure.'

'I see. Thank you, doctor.' The commander helped Elfrieda to her feet and turned to leave the room.

'By the way,' said the doctor. 'It was jolly bad luck, but it's your own fault. You really ought to use an axe or a meat cleaver next time. If you're going to do the job, you might as well do it properly.'

'Er. . .yes. Thank you, doctor.'

The commander and George took Elfrieda the dozen or so miles to the casualty department of the local hosital where she was X-rayed. A young Asian doctor examined the plates. 'No, there doesn't seem to be anything broken, although I would recommend a day or two in bed in case of concussion. You ought to try shooting her, or use a knife next time.'

'I beg your pardon?' said the commander icily.

'A sledgehammer is dangerous. You might easily hurt yourself. Hit yourself on the knee or something.'

'How dare you insinuate such a thing!'

The doctor patted the commander consolingly on the shoulder.

'I know how disappointed you must feel. Better luck next time.'

'Really!' exclaimed the commander, outraged.

It was a fortnight before he stopped being the butt of such merciless jokes. Bill even passed him some paraquat in the pub with a nod and a wink, saying that he knew how difficult it was to get hold of the stuff if one was not a proper farmer.

Elfrieda seemed in no great hurry to recover from her injury. The commander was quite worried about her. Not only did she show little enthusiasm for spreading the 10 tons of horse manure that he bought from the hunt, but she also took to reading strange magazines: *Spare Rib* and the *Spectator*, according to Maud at the post office. She was as silent as ever when she visited the pub, but she cut off most of her hair and took to wearing granny spectacles. And then she disappeared.

The pub noticed.

'You've managed it this time, commander. Well done,' said Bill.

'As long as you did not stick her in my slot in the churchyard,' added Jimmy.

'Where's she gone then, commander?' questioned Kelvin.

'She's just gone up to stay near Newbury for a few days.'

'Gone to Greenham Common?' asked Dennis with a laugh.

'As a matter of fact, she has,' replied the commander stiffly.

There was a short silence.

'Good God!' exclaimed Ivor.

'Good for her,' said Malcolm Jarrett, who had the *Guardian* delivered each morning.

'What do you mean by that?' blared out Kelvin, whose daughter read out the leader column of the *Sun* to him over breakfast. 'Those women are nothing but scum, tying up police time and going against what most people want anyway.' Kelvin, as well as looking forward to nuclear war when he was officially empowered to take over command of the village, was more right-wing than a barracuda and had all the *tendresse* of a drake mallard towards females.

'Are you calling my wife "scum"?' bristled the commander.

Kevin realized that his remark might have been construed as fairly rude. 'I wasn't talking about your Elfrieda. I meant those women that you see on the television, all dirty and making Indian war whoops.'

'Those women, as you call them, at least have the guts to turn their lives upside down in order to fight for something in which they believe,' replied the commander, showing what power love can bring to bear on the most unlikely characters, even *Daily Telegraph* readers.

Ivor and Dennis shot him a look of sympathetic understanding.

'Why exactly has she gone to Greenham?' asked Ivor. 'I never thought she'd be that way inclined. She always struck me as such a solid sensible woman.'

The commander spread out his hands in resignation. 'Search me. She'd never mentioned nuclear bombs before in her life. She even wanted me to work on a nuclear submarine once. But she dressed up in her potato-picking jeans and took the car and was off. She didn't even leave me anything in the oven. I don't know what's come over her. She's been behaving very oddly since she hit her head on my sledgehammer.'

'Yes, it does take some women that way,' said Dennis.

'What else has she been doing?' asked Bill. This was raw gossip, straight from the horse's mouth, so to speak, and thus more precious than rubies. It was only devalued by being delivered in front of an audience, thus immediately becoming part of the common currency.

'Well, she didn't do a wash last week. When I asked her for a shirt, she told me to look up the instructions in the washing-machine book. And she said that I was a bit of an old bore the other day. For some reason, that was even worse than being called a bore or an old bore. "A bit of an old bore" seemed to be sort of wet as well as boring.'

'How old is Elfrieda?' asked Dennis.

'She must be forty-eight, I suppose. It just goes to show how dangerous a crack on the head can be.'

'I wouldn't worry, old chap,' reassured Dennis. 'I don't think it's anything to do with that. I think it's probably the change of life.'

'What the hell is that supposed to mean?' asked Kelvin. His wife had scurried gratefully off to Abraham's bosom when she had been in her thirties, so it was understandable that Kelvin, not being a reader of women's magazines, had not come across the expression.

'It comes when a woman reaches a certain stage of her life and her hormonal balance changes,' said Dennis.

'Sort of like an identity crisis?' asked Kelvin.

'Well, yes. It often does involve an identity crisis. I wouldn't have thought you would know about that sort of thing.' Dennis was rather surprised. Crises of identity are one of the luxuries of the twentieth century and Kelvin's knowledge of modern human psychology could have been written on the head of a pin.

'Prudence bottle-reared a lamb a couple of years ago and it thought it was a dog. I had to get the vet out to it and he said that it was probably suffering from an identity crisis.'

Elfrieda spent a week up at Greenham. To the commander's mortification she was arrested for obstruction, which led to an extraordinary meeting of the committee of the local Conservative branch, of which she was a member, where it was agreed that she would not be asked to renew her subscription nor would she be invited to the wine and cheese party at which our MP was to be present. Elfrieda was totally oblivious to this pointed snub. She was embarking on a new life. When she came home, she ignored the commander's plaintive request that she cook him some dinner and went to visit the communards instead.

As mentioned earlier, the communards dwelt a mile or two outside the village in an enormous decaying mansion where they lived out an alternative lifestyle. To most of the villagers, who looked on their antics with a bemused but tolerant eye, all they seemed to have in common was a shared love of squalor and soya-bean cutlets. There were about a dozen adults currently in residence, with roughly the same number of children, and neither parents nor offspring seemed entirely sure who belonged to whom. The communards lived quite nicely on the proceeds of the social security cheques that wafted through their letterbox and were able to prevent even the remotest possibility of being asked to take a job by giving their occupations as astrologer, ley-line researcher or meditative therapist, none of which was much in demand at the local job centre.

Elfrieda had to wait a while before she got to speak to them because they were having a meeting with their sex therapist. This was a weekly event since the stress of living as sexually free agents led to all sorts of bourgeois emotions like jealousy and insecurity which they had thought they had left behind them in Esher and Neasden and all the other places whence they had come. The centre of the commune lay in the kitchen, which had a great deal in common with the ordinary farmhouse kitchen of a century earlier. There was an enormous old black iron cooking range over which were hung various clumps of drying herbs, most of which were legal. The floor was covered with flagstones, and what would otherwise have been an echoingly empty chamber, not unlike an old main-line railway-station public urinal, was dominated by 30 feet of kitchen table, cluttered with pots of home-made chutneys and jams and with a couple of dozen rickety chairs gleaned in batches of four from the local auction rooms lining its sides.

Elfrieda pushed her way through the front door and entered this kitchen, avoiding the old sitting room which lay at the front of the house and from which much wailing and passionate sobbing showed that everyone was having a wonderful time revealing their innermost fears and anxieties to the therapist. One wall of the kitchen was covered with notices advertising weekend courses in massage, alternative technologies and the politics of lesbianism. There were batches of magazines applicable to the lifestyle of the commune and with these Elfrieda occupied herself until the weekly purgative session should be completed. At intervals small and dirty-faced children would peer at her round the door or come into the kitchen and make unpleasantly precocious remarks about her age and the consequent deleterious effect of it upon her shape. One even told her that she looked like a llama which she absently corrected to camel.

The meeting in the next room ended with a burst of clapping which followed one of the members of the commune recalling his first significant sexual experience when his mother had lifted his penis as she had been changing his nappy. Then the communards came exuberantly through into the kitchen. This was the first time that Elfrieda had actually been inside the house, although she had attended the annual barbecue which was held in the stableyard at the back. The communards paused suspiciously when they saw her. Elfrieda, in spite of her short hair and specs, still looked like an ex-naval officer's wife. They were used to free spirits as visitors whose dog-like acceptance of every idea and belief that was put forward was only equalled by the equally doggy odour when one was downwind of them. Elfrieda looked as if she paid taxes.

Their visitor was equally uneasy. She had had no trouble in

associating with strangers at Greenham, but these were familiar strangers who had her pigeon-holed in a particular slot. Moreover, she did not know them individually. Nobody in the community did except for Dick who had once been in their midst. The communards all looked much the same, wearing similar drab clothes, and when they appeared in public one tended to look at their dirty toes poking out of their sandals or at their chests in an attempt to ascertain their sex: one did not look at their faces and, consequently, they were as indistinguishable from each other as traffic wardens.

'Oh hullo,' said one communard. He wore a straggly beard.

'I do hope that you don't mind me bursting in like this,' said Elfrieda, 'but the front door was wide open and I did not want to interrupt your meeting. You seemed to be having such fun.'

Communards do not have fun. It was something that Elfrieda ought to have known and it showed her essential naivety to have said what she did. Fun is frivolous and alternative livers take themselves desperately seriously.

The communard frowned in disapproval. 'We were exploring our unconscious.'

'How very interesting,' said Elfrieda politely. 'I was wondering if you would like to join the CND.'

'What?'

'I suppose I was a little abrupt,' said Elfrieda with a small laugh which sounded like the sand shifting under a camel's hoof. 'But I've just come back from Greenham Common and it struck me that there was no branch of the Campaign for Nuclear Disarmament in the village and that somebody ought to start one up.'

The communards looked at Elfrieda with rather more interest than before. 'You've been to Greenham?' asked one of them incredulously. Elfrieda did not fit into the popular conception of a Greenham woman but one would have hoped that the communards would have been above such prejudices.

'Yes.'

'Gosh!' Communards liked to think about things and even think about doing things, but they very rarely actually did

that Elfrieda was getting back to normal, although it was noted that there was a gleam of intelligence in her eye which was not part of her pre-sledgehammer look. Her dress had changed as well. Before she had been flattened by the bolt from the briny, she had gone in for twinsets and pearls; now she wore loose kaftans and headscarfs, while her feet were usually shod in a pair of old tennis shoes. The squire had informed Percy the policeman that he had seen a strange woman going into their house when he had first spotted her in her new rigout.

Elfrieda acknowledged the uneasy greetings from the resident fauna with a vague smile and ploughed her way through to her husband's side to engage him in earnest conversation. There was some relief that she appeared to be taking on her old responsibilities once more, especially when the commander began to become agitated at the prospect of being torn away from his booze and shook his head

things. They all looked at Elfrieda with wary respect.

'Well?' demanded Elfrieda. 'Will you join?'

The communards looked at each other uneasily. 'How many members have you got already?' asked one of them, who was already wearing a CND badge.

'None.'

'So it's not a very big group, then?'

'Not at the moment. But there's no reason why it shouldn't become one. After all, Christianity started off with only one man.'

'Yeah. That's right. So it did.'

'So will you join, then?'

The communards continued to shift uneasily from foot to foot. 'We don't really believe in joining things.'

'But you do believe in nuclear disarmament?'

'Oh, sure. And the banning of nuclear power and going back to a simpler way of life.'

'So if I organize a meeting or a demonstration, you might be willing to come to it?'

The communards looked at each other again. They did not seem to think individually, but by osmosis. What one knew or did not know seemed to be shared with all the others without the need for speech. If such a gift could have been shared by statesmen or scientists rather than communards, the human race would transform its condition almost overnight.

'Yeah,' was the eventual reply from the CND badge wearer who seemed to be the leader in this matter.

Elfrieda had to be satisfied with that. As part of her new lifestyle, she had bought herself a racing bicycle with which to travel round the neighbourhood. It was not the safest way of getting about, for she had not used a bike for at least three decades and, on the intricate cat's cradle of lanes that meandered from farm to farm, the ideal mode of transport would have been a tank with a permanently wailing siren to warn other vehicles of one's approach round the blind corners and to provide adequate protection when one met the inevitable deaf, drunk, retired colonel in a Land Rover coming in the opposite direction. Elfrieda rode home from the as long as the communards don't have anything catching.'

Kelvin was aghast. 'She can't do one of those marches in the village.'

'I think she's going to,' replied the commander.

'But I'm head of the emergency volunteers,' said Kelvin.

Dennis looked at him doubtfully. 'Isn't that a *non sequitur*?'

'No, it's a Dubonnet and blackcurrant. It makes a change from beer.'

'No, I mean what have the volunteers got to do with the CND? You surely don't think she wants to take over your job,' said Dennis.

' 'Course she couldn't take over my job,' replied Kelvin. 'She's a woman. But it's downright unpatriotic to want to get rid of our bombs. And anyone who joins the march is a traitor.'

'That's a bit strong, Kelvin,' protested the commander mildly. 'Unilateral disarmament may be considered by many to be unwise but disarmament itself, if the Russians get rid of theirs as well, is in all our interests.'

'Of course, that's a bit different. I mean if the Russians said they would get rid of theirs as well, then we could just pretend to get rid of ours and blow them to bits.'

'I'm not sure that that is the point,' murmured Dennis.

'Anyway, if people like Elfrieda get their way and we get rid of all our weapons, then all the work I've done to prepare fertilizer bags full of soil to put round my cattle sheds and making our cellar into a bomb shelter will have been for nothing. If there's no war, then there would be no point in having the emergency volunteers. And all that money that we've been spending on submarines and missiles and things like that will have been wasted.'

'I see what you mean,' said Dennis thoughtfully.

The commander was not going to allow Kelvin to get depressed. 'Come on, Kelvin. It won't be that bad. If Elfrieda's lot got their way and we did disarm, then the Russians could do as you suggested and drop their own bomb on us quite safely. So you'd still get to use your shelter and everything else.'

Kelvin was not to be mollified. If Elfrieda was going to organize a demo in the village, he was going to organize a counter-demo. He had had a red telephone extension installed in his cellar, which he referred to as his command line, and he sped home to muster his troops for the coming conflict.

The morrow dawned bright and clear. The village had never had a demo before, so there was considerable interest in what was to come. It might have been wiser had the commander biffed his wife in the autumn rather than late spring, because that would have meant that she would have organized a winter demo, when there would not have been any tourists around, rather than a summer one.

The pub was full at lunchtime. Word had got round the neighbourhood that there was to be some excitement that afternoon and the surrounding countryside had emptied as everyone came in to make sure that they did not miss any of the fun. Ninety per cent of the locals were either self-employed or retired so pleased themselves whether they worked or not. Most entertainment took the form of whist drives and slide lectures that were announced beforehand in the local papers; this was a genuine spontaneous happening.

It was all due to begin at 2pm down at the bridge, according to the commander who had come into the pub for some Dutch courage before the march got under way. He had just started on his third barley wine and was beginning to feel more calm in his mind when the pub door opened, letting in a stream of sunshine, Kelvin and Gary Loosemire.

Kelvin looked ferocious. He was wearing his wellies, since they were the closest thing he had to jackboots, and dark glasses and carried a walkie-talkie radio. Master Loosemire followed in his rear in similar garb. Kelvin strode over to the commander and stood beside him with his legs slightly apart and his hands behind his back. He was carrying a swagger stick with which he was tapping his gumboot.

'What's the procedure, then?' he asked briskly.

The commander looked at him suspiciously. 'I'm not sure that I ought to tell you,' he said. 'After all, you are the enemy.'

'If you don't tell me, I'll make you join the volunteers.'

'Don't be silly. I'd refuse. After all, I've already resigned once. I'll tell you if you buy me a drink.'

'Agreed,' said Kelvin without hesitation. 'Well?'

'I'll have the drink first,' said the commander.

'Don't you trust me?' asked Kelvin indignantly.

'Certainly not. I'll have a large scotch.'

'You're joking. I'm not going to buy you a large scotch. You can have a barley wine like you always do. I'm not going to have you in this demonstration inflamed with alcohol.'

Kelvin invested in a barley wine amid total silence from the rest of the customers who had been struck dumb by the sight of him buying a drink for someone else. The commander took a large draught and smacked his lips. A freebie always tastes nicer than anything one has had to pay for oneself.

'Right. Elfrieda has told me to report to the bridge at 2pm and then we're going to march up to the church hall and hold a meeting. Everyone is asked to come. I don't honestly know what you'll be able to do.'

'We will counter-demonstrate,' replied Kelvin stoutly.

'How?'

'Well, like they do on the telly. Picketing and that,' said Kelvin rather uncertainly.

'Throw stones and yell?' asked Dennis.

'I'm not so sure about throwing stones, but we might yell a bit.'

'If you yell at me, I'll certainly yell back at you,' said the commander. 'You'll have to be jolly quick about it, though, because it won't take all that long to get to the hall. It's only a couple of hundred yards.'

We enjoyed a desultory conversation about the prospects of the skittle team in a forthcoming match against the Rose and Crown in the neighbouring village during the half-hour before the demo was due to start. Then Kelvin rousted out the commander and they went down to the bridge to begin the business of the afternoon. Most of the rest of us went along to watch.

It may have been a mistake to have the start at the bridge as it was crowded with milling tourists. A couple of coaches had just vomited forth their loads which were wandering aimlessly around in the road as they waited for a leader to emerge from their ranks who would pioneer the route to the souvenir shop and the ice-creams. Elfrieda was there, together with the vicar and the Jarretts, but there was no sign of the expected demo-fodder from the commune.

Kelvin's turn-out was rather better. The squire had brought along a couple of his shooting cronies and there was a whole gaggle of Loosemires, all of whom were members of the emergency volunteers. After the bomb, when the telephone lines had been knocked out, Kelvin was going to communicate with his troops and the outside world by CB radio, and this was the attraction of the organization to the Loosemires. Their radios allowed them to talk to each other when they were on poaching expeditions. Since most of their poaching took place on the squire's shoots, the two groups were standing a few icy yards apart, eyeing each other with dislike. They both greeted Kelvin's arrival with relief. So did the vicar.

'My dear Mr Morchard,' he gushed, 'I'm so glad that you have decided to join us. It's so important that the leaders of our community are seen to be concerned about the prospects of atomic warfare.'

Kelvin was delighted that his importance should be recognized, particularly in front of the squire. 'I feel that it's my duty, Vicar,' he said with a simple but modest smile.

'He's in charge of a counter-demonstration, Vicar,' interrupted the commander. This was not news to the Jarretts or Elfrieda, but it certainly was to the vicar.

'I don't quite understand,' he said in some bewilderment.

Elfrieda explained. 'That lot,' she said, indicating the squire and the rest of the volunteers, 'think that the bomb is a good thing and they have come along to harass us. Don't worry, though. We have the right on our side.'

'I was thinking, Elfrieda,' said Kelvin, 'that it might be a good idea if you marched up to the church hall and then came back down to the bridge and marched up again so as to spin it out a bit. Otherwise it will be a bit short.'

'Yes,' she agreed, 'that seems quite a good idea. Are all your people here?'

'I think so,' said Kelvin, looking round at them. 'But you seem a bit light.'

'I'm hoping that there might be a few more.'

'We could always ask some of these people,' said the squire, indicating the Loosemires, 'to join up with Elfrieda's lot just to pad them out a bit.'

'That's a good idea,' said Kelvin.

'Here, wait a minute,' said Jason. 'I'm against these damn socialists. I'm not marching with them.'

'You'll do what you're bloody well told,' retorted Kelvin, 'if you want to stay in the volunteers and keep your radio.'

There were rebellious mutterings from the underlings and they went over to sit on the bridge parapet with the customers from the pub while the leadership continued to discuss matters of procedure in the forthcoming event.

'What exactly are you going to do, Elfrieda?' asked Kelvin.

'Walk through the village shouting, "Ban the Bomb," I suppose.'

'What do you think we should do?'

'I haven't really thought about it. Let's see.' Elfrieda thought a bit. 'It would probably be best if you marched behind us shouting, "Keep the bomb." '

Kelvin considered this, as did the commander and the squire, the chief lieutenants. 'I think we should walk in front,' he said.

'That would be silly. It's you who are counter-demonstrating against us. It would look as if it was the other way round if you were in front.'

'Darling,' interrupted the commander, 'I'm quite willing to walk by your side, but I'll feel an awful fool if I have to shout slogans.'

'I quite agree,' said the squire. 'No gentleman goes around shouting in the street. It's just not done.'

This was a serious rebellion, and the whole march would have been aborted before it had got under way if the police had not intervened. Percy was the police. He spent his summer sunbathing behind his car in remote parts of the moor with his shirt off and, on cloudy days, he went bird watching instead. Despite his being unaccustomed to any kind of dramatic occurrence, it was clear to him that this gathering of the village establishment needed investigation.

Percy was a stout man in his fifties and he pondered his way across the bridge towards them. He touched his cap as he came up. 'Afternoon,' he said, looking around hopefully for enlightenment as to what was going on. Nothing was forthcoming. 'Is anything the matter?'

'No, nothing is the matter,' said the commander eventually. 'We're just trying to settle details of this march through the village.'

'March? What march? Nobody told me about any march.'

After her experiences at Greenham, Elfrieda was ill-disposed to representatives of the Establishment. 'We're about to have a march against the bomb, but I don't see that it is any of your business,' she said.

Percy had heard about her little accident with the sledge-hammer and its unfortunate consequences and he was prepared to give her some latitude because of her condition, but he was not going to accept a trouble maker.

'It is my business. Marching and demonstrating is against the law unless you have the permission of the chief constable. And you haven't got his permission, otherwise I would have heard about it. So I'm afraid I must ask you to move along.' Percy had to be professionally schizophrenic. With visiting tourists, he was said to be thoroughly policemanlike, right down to accepting into safe keeping fivers and tenners which had been 'found' by erring motorists. When it came to dealing with the locals, it was rather different. Percy was considered to be a cross between a gamekeeper, translator of government forms, odd-job man and receiver of complaints about one's neighbours. The last thing expected of him was that he should order locals about. The squire, the commander and Kelvin looked at him in surprise. Elfrieda, however, had recently had some experience of police in this sort of situation.

'You cannot interfere with the democratic rights of citizens to protest against the fascist policies of the state,' she announced.

'Er . . . quite,' agreed her husband.

'I'm sorry,' responded Percy, 'you have every right to protest, but you need the permission of the chief constable first. Anyway, if you ask me, it's a bit bloody daft to have a march here. What the hell's the point of it?'

'We're showing the people that there is an alternative to the horror and absurdity of nuclear weapons.'

'That's right,' agreed Kelvin, 'and we're showing them that they're a damn good thing.'

'Why don't you just write a letter to the *Gazette*?'

'But we're going to have a meeting in the church hall to found a peace branch in the village.'

'You'd get a lot more people turning up if you wrote a letter.'

'Well, we're going to do it this way,' said Elfrieda obstinately.

'No, you're not,' said Percy.

'Yes, we are.'

'If you do, I'll arrest you.'

From all the spectators except the Loosemires, there was a murmur of astonishment. We had seen policemen going about arresting people in television series and read about it in thrillers, but Percy was not a real policeman. He was the man who grew stunted onions which were always defeated by those of the commander or Jimmy for the Onion Shield at the horticultural show.

The squire cleared his throat. 'Excuse me, Constable.'

Everyone else called him Percy, but the squire was conscious of his position and felt it incumbent upon himself to retain the old standards.

So did Percy. He touched his cap. 'Afternoon, Squire.'

'Good afternoon, Constable. Don't you think that this fuss is a bit unnecessary?'

'I quite agree. But the law is the law and my job is to enforce it.'

'What about closing time, then?' said Kelvin. The pub closed when the last customer was shovelled out the door when Helga wanted to go to bed. It was the custom that Percy did not have to pay for his drinks should he still be in the bar after 11pm.

'That's different,' said Percy, refusing to be ruffled.

'Why?' demanded Kelvin.

'Because I say it is,' replied Percy, with magnificent and uncharacteristic confidence.

'Are you saying that this march can only proceed with the permission of the chief constable?' asked the squire.

'That's right, Sir.'

'In that case, I'll have a word with him.'

The squire swiftly moved towards the communal telephone box on the other side of the street. Percy, highly alarmed, pattered after him, accompanied by raucous noises from the Loosemires. Percy used to clatter but his feet had been giving him a hard time recently and he was wearing tennis shoes which his wife had dyed black. The square slammed the door behind him, leaving Percy hopping from one foot to the other outside. A tide of spectators crossed over to form a circle round them. Percy was trying to force open the door of the box, but the squire was holding it firmly shut. Not being a chicken, Percy was unable to run round in a circle clucking, but he was badly in need of some form of displacement activity. The spectators were spilling off the pavement on to the road and so he began to chivy at their edges. Nobody, not even he, took his efforts seriously, but it gave him an occupation while the squire made contact with his supreme commander.

The squire poked his head round the door. 'Henry would like a word with you, Constable.'

Percy turned white. The Loosemires jeered. 'Go on, Percy. Go and speak to Henry. There's a good boy.'

Percy rounded on them. 'Shut up, you lot.' He straightened his tie and marched towards the receiver which the squire was holding out to him through the door of the telephone box. He took it in a hand which had a distinct tremor and went inside closing the door firmly behind him. The crowd pressed against the glass but, maddeningly, the conversation was inaudible.

'We might as well get going, then,' said Elfrieda.

'It might be best if we waited for Percy, dear,' replied her husband. 'Now that he's involved, it might look a bit more . . . er . . . professional if he's walking beside us. I mean, when you see any marches on the news, there are always policemen walking along beside them.'

'You're quite right,' said Elfrieda. 'We'll wait.'

The commander almost blushed. It was the first time that he had been right in the eyes of his wife since he had hit her over the head.

Percy came out of the kiosk and strolled across the road trying to look like the majestic guardian of the law that he was not. 'This is all most irregular,' he said. 'As I told the chief constable, it's just not good enough to have verbal permission. I have to have it in writing at least seven days before the event takes place.'

'You mean that you're still going to try to stop us marching?' asked Kelvin.

'I didn't say that,' said Percy hastily, giving the squire a nervous look in case he made a beeline back across the road to the telephone. 'All I said is that you are supposed to give me at least a week's notice.'

'Why?' asked Elfrieda.

'Why?' repeated Percy. 'It's obvious, isn't it? So that we have time to draft in police reinforcements for crowd and traffic control and that sort of thing. There might be clashes between rival groups and we have to be prepared to prevent civil disorder by keeping the two sides apart. One of those big demonstrations like they have in London would be more than one man could control.'

'You're not going to try to keep us apart?' asked Kelvin.

'That's my job,' replied Percy, with the simple air of a man who knows his duty.

'But we want to march together.'

'Well, you can't. You might riot. The chief constable said that it was up to me as the man on the spot to decide how best to handle the situation and I say you can't march together.'

'You're not being very helpful,' said the commander mildly.

'It's your own fault. You shouldn't have gone ahead and organized something like this without letting me know about it in advance. It doesn't make me look too good and I'm going to get blown up when my inspector finds out that I've been chatting on the telephone to the chief. Anyway, I wish you'd hurry up and get going. My wife has got freshly made scones for tea and I don't want to hang around here all day.'

'All right, all right,' said Elfrieda and, with her husband by her side, and the massed ranks of her supporters – all five of them – following behind, she began to lead the procession on its way. Afterwards came Percy and, a couple of yards behind him, Kelvin and his men. There was one more anti than there was pro and so Lindy was prevailed upon to come out of the crowd to join the protesters. Elfrieda raised her arm like a US 7th Cavalry captain leading his troopers out of the fort for a dangerous patrol amid the Apaches, and the village's first political demonstration and counter-demonstration were under way.

'Ban cruise missiles!' yelled Elfrieda as she cleared the car park at the head of the procession and entered the street.

'Shh, you're embarrassing me,' muttered the commander as the tourists turned to look with the blank, bovine gaze with which all tourists view the world around them.

Elfrieda's reply was drowned by the stentorian tones of Kelvin.

'Support the Independent British Nuclear Deterrent!' he bellowed.

Elfrieda flung her arm in the air. 'Stop!' The procession stopped. She left her place at its head and walked back to Kelvin. 'If you must shout something out, at least make sure it's accurate,' she said.

'What's wrong with that?' replied Kelvin, rather hurt. 'It's not easy to say "Independent British Nuclear Deterrent". I thought I had said it rather well.'

'I don't deny the quality of your diction. But cruise missiles are under American control.'

'Oh,' replied Kelvin, somewhat deflated. 'Does that matter?'

The squire came to his aid. 'He didn't mention anything about missiles. He could have been referring to submarines or bombers. All he's saying is that he supports the British deterrent.'

'Yeah. That's right,' agreed Kelvin.

'This demonstration is against cruise missiles,' said Elfrieda.

'So you say,' replied Kelvin. 'Your demonstration may be against cruise missiles. But that doesn't mean that ours has to be.'

'I'm not suggesting that it has to be against them. We disagree. But if you're holding a counter-march it ought to counter us, not talk about something totally different.'

'Why?'

'Why? Well, it's silly. You might as well walk behind us shouting "Votes for women" or "Keep Britain tidy".'

Kelvin thought about that for a few seconds. 'Why should we shout "Votes for women"?' It took incomers years to learn to appreciate and cope with the remarkable literalness of the locals' manner of thought. Elfrieda had lived in the village for only a few years and still tended to forget that natives thought with the logical simplicity of computers.

'For heaven's sake! I'm not suggesting you should. All I'm saying is that if you have to tag along behind us, at least be relevant. Otherwise go away and have your own demonstration.'

Kelvin was miffed. 'If you're not going to appreciate us, we'll bloody well do just that.' He turned round to his troops. 'Come on, lads. We'll go back to the car park and wait for this lot to get well away and then we'll have our own march.'

Percy was not going to put up with that. 'You will bloody well do nothing of the sort. The chief constable said it was up to me to maintain order and I can't be in two places at once. If you want to march, you march behind Elfrieda.' He turned to higher authority for help. 'Squire, you tell him.'

The squire was not playing. 'It's nothing to do with me, Constable. In this situation, I just take orders from my superior officer.'

'And that's me,' said Kelvin.

Percy sighed heavily. 'Kelvin, your tractor hasn't got a licence. The MOT has run out. It's got a bald front tyre. You've got ragwort rampant in one of your fields. You've got an unlicensed dog. You leave the public highway in a muddy and dangerous condition every time you drive your cows across it and I'm sure the water authority would like to know that it was you who released all that slurry into the river a couple of weeks ago. So I suggest you march along behind me nice and peaceably. And quietly. If you don't shout anything, then Elfrieda won't either. Isn't that right, Elfrieda?'

'I'm sorry, but I can't agree to police dictates like that.'

'Yes, you can,' interrupted the commander. 'If you shout anything out, you're on your own. Me and the vicar will leave you to march by yourself. Isn't that right, Vicar?' That was right by the vicar.

With that incipient rebellion quashed, Elfrieda took her place at the head of the procession once again and it moved out from the car park on to the road and began the long march to victory. It became apparent quite quickly that there was a problem. Without the freedom to shout, the demonstration did not look much like a demonstration. There were at least one hundred tourists in the village – two coachloads and a stiffening of car travellers – and all they saw were a dozen or so people rather foolishly walking on the road instead of the pavement and another bunch, the pub customers, walking behind them. They did look a bit odd; none of them, for example, was sucking an ice-cream or wearing nylon shorts and, instead of the discreet day-glo reds, blues and yellows that the tourists favoured, they wore browns, greens and the muted colours of the countryside. The whole procession was forced to skip on to the pavement when a luxury busload of Germans fanfared its way up the street before coming to a stop as a small horse and its young rider, obviously hot favourites for the Thelwell class in the gymkhana the following week, skittered in fright in front of it.

'This is not working very well,' said Elfrieda, dissatisfied, as they stood on the pavement in the great shadow cast by the side of the bus as it throbbed impatiently, waiting for the obstruction in front of it to clear so that it could move on and envelop the pedestrians in clouds of black smoke from its exhaust. 'Kelvin!' she had to shout to make herself heard above the engine of the coach, 'come here!'

Kelvin shouldered his way through the tourists and his followers who were hemmed in by the bus. 'What we need are banners. If we held up banners as we marched, then there would be no doubts as to what we represented.'

'Where are we going to get banners from, Elfrieda?'

'Where do all these posters come from that advertise the flower show and the jumble sales?'

'You buy the blanks from the post office and fill in the words yourself.'

'Let's do it, then,' said Elfrieda crisply.

The procession moved quickly across the street, Percy kindly holding up his hand in front of the traffic which was not going anywhere since the pony had decided that it was more fun to practise its pirouettes in front of the bus than to risk squeezing between it and the parked cars that lined the other side of the street. There were a couple of tourists already in the post office, buying stamps to stick on their postcards, but they were easily swept aside.

'Posters, please, Maud,' demanded Elfrieda.

'That'll be £1.60, please,' said the shopkeeper, handing over the goods.

'Give her the money, dear,' said Elfrieda to her husband.

'I don't see why I should,' objected the commander. 'This business is not my idea so I don't see why I should have to pay.'

'I haven't got my handbag with me,' said Elfrieda patiently.

'You pay then, Kelvin.'

'I'm not paying for anything,' said Kelvin hurriedly.

'If you don't pay, I won't give you any of the posters,' warned Elfrieda.

'Maud, you'll let me charge a packet of posters, won't you?' asked Kelvin confidently. Maud was part of his mafia. Established villagers were either the Montagues of Kelvin, or the Capulets of Bill, although there was some blurring where an individual was equally related to both of them. Maud was only Bill's second cousin, whereas she was twice a cousin of Kelvin and the sister of his late wife.

'No,' said Maud.

'Go on. I'll be able to reclaim the money from the government or the Ministry of Defence. After all, we're doing their job for them, demonstrating against a demonstration.'

'No,' repeated Maud.

Percy intervened at this point. 'Maud, do us a favour, love. Give them the sodding posters, otherwise this business is going to take all day.'

Maud softened, giving Percy a smile. She was quite fond of

him as he generated a good deal of business for her by chasing up out-of-date licences for TVs and cars. 'No,' she said.

Percy sighed and pulled out his wallet. 'Okay, but give me a receipt, please, although I've no idea how I'll get the money back.'

The demonstrators looked on with satisfaction as Maud counted out his change. 'Has anyone got a felt pen?' asked Elfrieda.

Percy sighed again and purchased four of them. The demonstrators shooed out the tourists who were beginning to back up into the street in their quest for stamps, spread the blank sheets of paper over the floor and began to fill in their slogans.

The antis had it easy: 'Ban the bomb', 'Ban Cruise missiles' and 'Send Maggie on a Cruise' they wrote, and filled out the rest with some rather uncertainly drawn CND symbols. Kelvin went into a huddle with the squire and they conferred for some time before they came over to see how the opposition was doing.

'I was wondering if you had any ideas about what we should put on our posters,' said Kelvin hesitantly to Elfrieda.

'You know, Kelvin, you've really got a blasted nerve. You not only muck up my march, but you expect me to help muck it up for you.'

'If it wasn't for me, you wouldn't have a bloody march. There wouldn't be anyone here.'

'Do you know, that's a very good point,' said the squire. 'If we go home and leave Elfrieda by herself, we'll have won.'

'You wouldn't!' cried Elfrieda in horror.

'Why not?' said the squire, looking smug.

'I'll tell you why not,' said Kelvin. 'Because I'm enjoying myself. That's why not.'

'And because I've spent £2.20,' agreed Percy, 'and if you cancel the march, I won't have a chance in hell of getting my money back. Anyway the chief constable is now expecting a march and there'll be hell to pay if we don't give him one. So you keep your law-abiding ideas to yourself, Squire, if you don't mind.'

With the squire crushed, Kelvin and Elfrieda put their collective minds to the problem of the right slogans.

'Nuke the Russkies?' suggested Kelvin.

'It's a bit crude,' replied Elfrieda critically. 'What was it that you were shouting earlier on?'

'Support the British Independent Nuclear Deterrent?'

'That's right. How about that?'

'I thought you didn't approve of that.'

'Oh, nor I did, but I don't suppose it really matters.'

Kelvin started to write. He got halfway through before he started to worry. 'How do you spell "deterrent"?'

'One "t" and two "rs".'

'And is it "ant" or "ent"?'

' "Ent".'

He continued to write, breathing heavily through his mouth as he concentrated. 'There isn't enough room to get it all in.'

'Well, use the back too.'

It took Kelvin a long time as calligraphy was not his forte, and to speed things up everyone lent a hand. It was an odd selection that he ended up with: 'We want the bomb', 'The bomb puts the 'B' in Britain'. There was some discussion about 'Maggie deserves her Cruise' but it was felt that there was some ambiguity about it. His own said 'Support the British' on the front and 'Independent Nuclear Deterrent' on the back.

Eventually all was done and the procession vacated the post office and returned to the street. It was one of the disadvantages of the village that once the traffic stopped it tended to stay stopped. A large vehicle in the centre or on the bridge faced by another large vehicle meant that one of them would have to reverse extremely quickly before traffic built up behind it. This left a problem for Percy. One of his main duties was to keep the local arteries from furring up but, as we all know, once they had done so, it was a virtual impossibility for anything except time to flush them out. He took a swift look outside the door of the post office and dived back inside.

'Can I use your back door, Maud?'

'What's wrong? Has the traffic seized up again?'

'I'm afraid so. It looks like a bad one, too.'

Elfrieda was not going to allow this. 'Percy! What do you think you're up to? I'm not letting you sneak off somewhere. Your job is to escort our demonstration and make sure that there's no trouble.'

'You wanted rid of me a few minutes ago.'

'I know, but I reckon a policeman adds a certain *gravitas* to something like this.'

'If I go out there, it won't be to escort you. I'll be sorting out cars from now until supper time. There's no easy way of doing that job.'

'You mean no easy way of skiving,' said Kelvin.

'That's right. So I've found that it's a lot easier if I just make myself scarce when it gets like this. That bus is driven by a foreigner too and I've found that it is bad enough trying to get them to drive on the right side of the road but bloody nearly impossible to get them to manage it going backwards. So I'm nipping out Maud's back door and going home for my tea. It's—'

'—Scones and clotted cream. I know, you told us,' finished Elfrieda.

'So bye-bye, then. Enjoy yourselves.' He nipped behind the counter and was gone along a route that he had obviously travelled many times before, behind the pub and across a couple of garden fences before cutting beneath the bridge, well out of sight of the passing populace and back up to the policeman's cottage to his cream tea.

Elfrieda sighed. 'Right. I suppose it's time we got on with it.'

The protesters got under way once again. There were plenty of tourists on the pavements, but the road was clear the 50 or so yards between the busload of tourists and the hay wagon. Many tourists stopped to watch as Elfrieda lined up her marchers on the roadway.

'Ho Ho Ho Chi Minh!' she shouted, right in the faces of a couple of startled Americans who must have wondered if they had ventured into a time warp.

The commander cracked. 'Right!' he said. 'That's it. I warned you that if you started shouting then I was off. Take this damn poster!' He thrust one of the posters – 'Ban the bum', it said with a surprisingly good image of Reagan on it – into Elfrieda's hands and stalked off down the street, past the German bus, ignoring his wife's despairing cry to come back. He was warmly received back into the bosom of the pub customers who were idling their time away a little further down the pavement, waiting for something interesting to happen. One of them had thoughtfully brought along a bottle of barley wine, the commander's favourite tipple, and he gratefully poured it down his throat, turning his back on the political event. Elfrieda's procession was in danger of haemorrhaging away. Without Percy and the commander, it had lost twenty per cent of its available strength and the bulk of Kelvin's supporters, the Loosemires, were only hanging on by a thread.

Elfrieda had learned something about organization in the past week or two. Only herself and Kelvin were fully committed to their causes and so they amalgamated. Elfrieda stayed at the front to lead and Kelvin remained at the back to prevent anyone else making a break for it. During the confusion as they sorted themselves out, the squire managed to abandon the leaking ship by slipping back into the post office, ostensibly to check on Christmas posting dates for sending smoked salmon to some relation in New Zealand.

Elfrieda's troubles were far from over. She had just re-mustered the few protesters that remained and was inspecting the banners that were unfurled, ensuring that those held by her supporters masked, as far as possible, those held by Kelvin's, when Jimmy came tacking down the street towards her, carving a wide path through the tourists whom he ignored as he would a flock of sheep that were blocking his way. Jimmy had bandy legs, giving him a rolling gait which pitched him violently to starboard at every second pace when he would thrust out a knobbly blackthorn stick which stopped him falling into the road. If there was anyone in the way of the stick, that was their bad luck.

Jimmy pulled his limbs into a stationary position as he came towards Elfrieda and surveyed her little group. He had not been in the pub over the past few days since his rheumatics had been playing him up and he had therefore not been aware of the demonstration. He had also been quaffing large quantities of elderflower wine at home, and it showed. His mood had not been improved when he had heard that there was a busload of Germans in the village: he had come to have a look to ensure that Martin Bormann was not on board.

'What's all this, then?' he asked suspiciously.

'We're demonstrating,' replied Elfrieda, with a certain degree of satisfaction, since Jimmy was the first member of the general public to enquire and there was very little point in demonstrating if nobody knew that one was doing so.

'What are you demonstrating?' asked Jimmy.

Elfrieda thought about that for a few seconds. 'It's not what we're demonstrating. It's why we're demonstrating.'

It was Jimmy's turn to think. 'I went to a demonstration the other day. It was run by the Ministry of Agriculture and they were demonstrating sheep dip. Sheep dip was the what, and the why, I suppose, was that it was their job.'

'Ah, but that was a different sort of demonstration. This is a sort of parade. We're against the Cruise missiles.'

'Is that right?' asked Jimmy. He looked at the odd assortment of folk behind her. 'And what's Cruise missiles?'

'They're a new way of delivering nuclear bombs.'

Jimmy shook his head. 'That's terrible, isn't it? Them bloody Russians will get up to anything. All the same, I don't see much point in walking through the village waving bits of paper in the air. You'd have more chance if you wrote to our MP and told him that we ought to have some ourselves. You'd think the bloody Americans would have a few. They're always piss useless when it comes to the crunch.'

'But that's the whole point, Jimmy,' said Elfrieda patiently. 'It's not the Russians who have the missiles. It's the Americans and they've stationed them in this country.'

Jimmy looked disgusted. 'They're threatening us with them? I always knew those bloody Yanks were not to be trusted. They want our women and they always have done.'

Elfrieda, had she been of a lesser breed, might have considered giving up at this point, but she was a graduate of Greenham and there can be few tougher training schools in the world. 'You don't understand, Jimmy. The Americans are threatening the Russians with these missiles. They are part of the NATO deterrent.'

'You mean that they're our missiles?'

'Well, not exactly ours. The Americans control them.'

'But they're not aimed at us, they're aimed at the Russians?'

'They're certainly supposed to be used against the Russians in the event of war.'

Jimmy chewed this information over before deciding that it called for some action. 'In that case, you're a disgrace to your country. Excuse me, ladies.' Jimmy must have been drinking rather more than usual, for he proceeded to step round Elfrieda and Lindy and wade into the male demonstrators behind them. He got in one blow against Kelvin but Jason Loosemire ducked, causing him to overbalance and fall down on the pavement.

It was bad luck on Elfrieda. By the time she and Lindy had got him to his feet and brushed him down, her fellow demonstrators had disappeared, abandoning their posters all over the road. Even Kelvin had given up in disgust in the face of the busload of Germans who had disembarked with their cameras clicking like typewriters to preserve this authentic slice of English rural behaviour. With the tourists following a wary 20 yards behind her, Elfrieda picked up one of her posters and trailed up to the church hall on her own for the meeting, but the door was locked. It was not her day.

She managed to achieve something out of the debacle, however. The commander was stricken with guilt and, at the next meeting of the parish council, he proposed that the village be declared a nuclear-free zone. It was carried, with Kelvin providing the sole dissenting vote.

Chapter Seven

ARTHUR MEE, in his monumental work *King's England*, described our parish as being 'remote and lost in the high moorland'. Daniel Defoe had journeyed nearby a couple of centuries earlier and had contented himself with a sour remark about the poverty of the land through which he had travelled. Before that, Celia Fiennes had considered the locals to be dirty and ill-mannered. About the only thing of interest that had ever occurred in the parish was the advent, during the nineteenth century, of a coach with a crest on the door which had deposited a young lady in the latter stages of pregnancy at the village inn. She and her child had both died in labour and still lay in the churchyard. The funeral had been paid for from a store of sovereigns found in her room after her death and her name had never been discovered. The legend, still mulled over when there was nothing more current to gossip about, held that part of the crest had been a ducal coronet.

In many ways, the village still seemed to be out on a limb. It lay at the junction of three parliamentary constituencies. The neighbouring parish was in the next county. We paid rates to two separate water boards and were ruled by a district council whose headquarters lay in a city an hour's drive away instead of in the town where everyone did their shopping and whose newspaper reported on the doings of the local hunts and the winners of whist drives and trophies at the horticultural show.

Because nobody bought the newspaper in which official events were reported, information, sometimes quite important official information, tended to pass us by. The commander was first to come across a rather critical example of this. It was about 4pm on a fine Thursday afternoon. Elfrieda was away for a couple of days at a seminar on the international role of women in nuclear disarmament. The commander now approved of her new interest, mainly because, at 4pm on a fine summer's day with her out of the way, it allowed him to snooze in front of the Test match with the curtains in his sitting room drawn instead of feeling obliged to slave away amid his cabbages and courgettes to keep the bank manager at bay.

Then there was a knock at the door. The commander's first thought was to slip through the French windows and out to the vegetables so that he would not be caught *in flagrante lethargo* by whoever was calling. He gave himself a quick lecture about being a man entitled to do as he pleased and how, in his retirement, he need no longer concern himself about what other people thought of him before padding to answer the door in his slippers. On the threshold was a small man in his fifties wearing a shiny suit and carrying a briefcase. He smiled apologetically at the commander who smiled politely back. It is very difficult to prevent this normal human reaction even if, as in this case, the commander had a nasty suspicion that the knocker might be an insurance salesman, if not a disguised Jehovah's Witness.

'Are you the man of the house?' asked his caller.

'If you must put it that way,' replied the commander. 'What can I do for you?'

'Do you have a television?'

'Ah!' said the commander, comprehension dawning. 'It's another collapse. Both Botham and Lamb are out.' The commander looked at his caller sympathetically. He must be a very dedicated afficionado to knock at the doors of strangers to find out the cricket score.

'So you have a set?'

'Yes, I've just said so. Would you like to come in and watch for a bit?'

'Thank you very much.'

The commander led his strange guest through into the living room where, in the gloom, burbled Messrs Laker and Benaud who were forced to shout to compete against the snores and farts from the commander's geriatric basset hound which lay on a stinking bean bag in a corner.

'Do you watch television regularly?' asked the caller.

'Well, fairly regularly. Not usually at this time of day, though. My wife's away,' explained the commander.

'May I see your television licence, please?'

The commander's blood turned to ice in his veins. That has got to be one of the most dreaded sentences of our age, comparable to 'I forgot to post the coupon' or, in earlier days,

'It looks like the plague' or 'Say now shibboleth'. 'Why?' he prevaricated.

'My name is Mr Harbottle. I am from the Post Office and we are checking licences in this area. It was announced in the local paper a couple of weeks ago.'

'Which paper?'

'The *Courier*.'

'Everyone round here takes the *Gazette*,' said the commander.

'Is that so? Well, we have no record of a licence being issued at this address so I would like to see it, please.'

'Ah!' replied the commander. 'You won't have a record because we've only recently moved in.'

'That would explain it then,' Mr Harbottle continued to look expectantly at the commander, who walked briskly out of the room towards the front door.

'If there's nothing else, I'll show you out. The match is at a critical stage.'

His visitor did not move. 'May I see your licence, please?' he repeated.

The commander was fighting a losing engagement in face of the mindless tenacity of a dedicated bureaucrat, but he had had not achieved rank in the service that still revered the memory of Nelson by retreating in the face of any enemy, even if the odds were overwhelming.

'I've a nasty feeling it may have got lost in the move,' said the commander optimistically.

'I see,' said Mr Harbottle. 'When did this move take place?'

'Only a year or two ago.' The commander was not so much skating on thin ice as trying to walk on water.

'The licence is issued annually.'

'Oh, is it? My wife must have renewed it, then. It must be in her desk somewhere. Hang on a second.'

Elfrieda's desk, unfortunately, was in the same room as the television. The commander shuffled through the papers in the drawers and pigeon holes, hoping for a miracle in that one of them might turn into the required document.

'It doesn't seem to be there,' observed Mr Harbottle

politely. 'I don't think you have got a current television licence, have you?'

The commander changed his tactics. 'I don't see why I should need one. The reception here is lousy.'

This was quite true. The signal had to travel many miles and it was often exhausted by the time it came to trickle down the sides of the hills that surrounded the village, often achieving little more than snowstorms and wavy lines on local sets.

'That's as may be,' said Mr Harbottle. 'This does not obviate the necessity of ensuring compliance with the Wireless Telegraphy Act of 1949.'

'What?'

'You still need a licence.'

The commander swivelled his gun turret, probing for a weak spot. 'I see no reason to pay for the sort of pap they put on these days. Apart from the cricket, there hasn't been anything worth watching since they took off *The Magic Roundabout*.'

'I sympathize with your point of view. My wife insists on watching *Dallas* and *Dynasty*.'

'How dreadful for you!'

Mr Harbottle gave a little shudder but recalled himself to his duty. 'However, I am an employee of the Post Office and not the BBC and you still need a licence. I am afraid I am going to have to report you and it will be up to my superiors whether they take the matter any further.'

The commander came into the pub that evening in a lather of concern. He was not the only person who had been visited. Ivor had been out making hay and had found a note from Mr Harbottle in his letterbox promising a return visit. He had been round most of the village and Kelvin had actually been forced to deny on his doorstep that he owned a TV set, claiming that the aerial had been installed as a perch for the housemartins that nested along the front of his house. The whole pub was behaving like a herd of zebras when a lion is in the vicinity, honking and whinnying in alarm and restlessly shifting about. After some heated discussion, there was a run on the post office the following day led by the commander, and Maud took enough to finance at least one episode of *The Sky at Night*.

For almost everyone, it was just a seven-hour wonder, a brief flurry of excitement that squalled its way through the even tenor of our ways before receding rapidly into the recesses of memory – nasty, but short. It became much more interesting a few weeks later when the commander received his summons through the mail. There was nothing that the village enjoyed more than a disaster happening to someone else. Frank Mattock drove everyone potty when he kept winning competitions, but the commander's popularity rose considerably when it was realized that he would be going before the courts. There was a heady whiff of doom, shame and disgrace emanating from him that allowed the rest of us to feel pleasantly secure and superior.

It was Kelvin, with his inimitable lack of subtlety, who expressed the general feeling of the community. 'You won't be able to go to America, you know, Commander.'

The commander looked up from his drink. 'Why ever not?'

'Because you'll have a criminal record,' replied Kelvin with relish. 'They're very particular about that sort of thing over there. They don't let riff-raff into their country.'

'Don't be silly. Not having a TV licence is like a parking offence. They don't mind about that sort of thing.'

'It's not quite the same thing as a parking offence,' said Bill. 'One's a footling bit of nonsense and the other . . . well, there's the intention to defraud.'

'Nonsense!' said the commander.

'I reckon it is. You've been watching things on TV which the rest of us have to pay for. It costs money to put things on the TV, you know. All those widows and orphans who pay their licence have been letting you watch it for free. You've been stealing from widows and orphans and that's a serious business.'

'That's right,' agreed Kelvin. 'Come to think on it, I'm an orphan, so I suppose you've been stealing from me.'

'For heaven's sake!' said the commander. 'I don't want to go to America. Anyway you're a fine one to talk, Kelvin, because you haven't got a licence yourself.'

'But they didn't catch me, did they?' crowed Kelvin.

The commander could normally stand up for himself, but he was oppressed by his forthcoming humilation. 'It's not bloody fair that they should pick on me. You know, they couldn't even get the date right on the summons. I think that that Mr Harbottle tricked me into letting him into the house. I've a good mind to fight the whole thing.'

'You hadn't got a licence, so you're guilty and there's no point in whingeing about it. You'll have to take your punishment like a man. I think they can fine you up to £400. And your shame will be reported in the paper.' Kelvin was really enjoying himself.

'Jesus!' said the commander despairingly.

'What do you mean, they got the wrong date on the summons?' asked Helga from across the bar.

'They dated the summons the day that Harbottle came out and put yesterday's date in the space where they should have put the other.'

There was a silence while everyone tried to work out what the commander was trying to say. Helga got there first. 'You mean they are summonsing you to appear for not having a TV licence the day before yesterday?'

'That's what it says.'

'But you bought a licence a month ago.'

'Yes.'

'But don't you see? You're not guilty then.'

Kelvin, in mid-sip, was seized by a violent coughing fit. His fellow drinkers looked at him with interest as he doubled over, spluttering beer on to the floor. He straightened and mopped his face with a large khaki handkerchief. 'What do you mean "not guilty"?' he said weakly. ' 'Course he's guilty. He didn't have a licence and he was nicked.'

'That's true, but it looks as though they may have charged him with the wrong thing. They're accusing him of not having a licence when he had one.'

'Well, I think it'll be a bloody scandal if he gets away with it.'

There were quite a few people of Kelvin's opinion. After all, where lies the pleasure in attending a hanging if the victim gets a reprieve on the scaffold? In spite of this, half a dozen went along to see the commander have his day in court, just on the off-chance that he might receive his come-uppance. He had taken the trouble to consult his solicitor and had been advised to hold his peace for as long as possible, because the further the prosecution got into his case, the less simple it would be for them to correct what was a minor clerical error.

The villagers filed into the benches at the back of the courtroom before the start of business. The commander looked most peculiar since he had put on a suit for the occasion and a white shirt which had been carefully ironed by Elfrieda before she had left to attend her consciousness-raising class.

The usher suddenly said, 'All rise,' and we scrambled to our feet as the three magistrates filed on to their platform and sat down.

'Christ!' muttered the commander. One could understand

why. The bench was occupied by a stout woman in her late forties who had stood as the Ecology Party candidate at the last general election, an extremely small and very old man with a bad cold, and the squire.

The last was a bit of a shock. At intervals news percolated round the community that the squire was in receipt of certain semi-hereditary honours: high sheriffdoms, deputy lieutenancies, council membership of the Country Landowners Association and as an adornment at the top of various local charities. It was alarming, however, to find a man of his calibre in a position of real power over the destiny of others, particularly since he was in the midst of one of his periodic attacks of gout, during which his outlook on the world was extremely malevolent.

It took Kelvin a minute or two to realize the identity of the third magistrate as he had been admiring a large-busted female solicitor near the front of the court. Then he clicked. 'Look who's there. It's the squire.' He waved his arms, shouting 'Yoo-hoo!' across the room.

The commander was not happy. 'For heaven's sake, behave, Kelvin!' he hissed. 'It's all very well for you, but I am dependent on the goodwill of that lot to the tune of £400.'

Kelvin was indignant. 'That's the squire up there. What's wrong with saying hullo to him? He's a friend of mine.' The commander had learned to whisper, but Kelvin had not.

'Silence in court,' said an official.

'It's all right,' replied Kelvin, nodding at him in a friendly fashion. 'The squire's up there, we know each other.' He turned his attention back to the squire. 'Didn't expect to see you here on a nice haymaking day like this,' he bellowed. 'Going to send the commander to jail, I hope.'

The chairperson looked annoyed, as did the usher who was unused to having his orders treated so lighly. The squire cast an outraged look in our direction and proceeded to erect a large pile of books in front of him which effectively obscured him from our sight. The chairperson found a gavel and thumped the desk. 'I must ask the public to remain silent.'

A black-leather-clad figure on the bench in front of Kelvin, probably up for biting the heads off chickens, turned round.

'Yeah. Shut your face, you silly old berk.'

Kelvin was not prepared to tolerate that. 'Who do you think you're talking to, you cheeky bastard? I'll have you know I used to be a special constable and I'm chairman of our branch of the emergency volunteers.'

'For Christ's sake, Kelvin,' moaned the commander as he slid along the bench to put as much distance between them as possible in order to dissociate himself.

'What's wrong with you?' demanded Kelvin. 'That cheeky sod called me a silly old berk. You heard him.'

The chairperson banged again. 'Sir,' she shouted. Kelvin looked enquiringly at her. 'It is customary, in fact it is compulsory, that those not involved in the business of the court should remain silent.'

'But—' started Kelvin.

'And even if you are involved in the business of the court, you should remain silent until you are spoken to.'

'Well, you are speaking to me,' said Kelvin reasonably.

'Be silent!' said the usher.

'Yeah,' said the leather jacket.

'And that goes for you too!'

'What the hell do you mean?' said the leather jacket angrily. 'I'm on your side.'

'You've never been on the side of anyone but yourself in your life, you damn yob,' flared Kelvin.

The commander was rocking himself backwards and forwards with his hands clasped between his knees. The angrier those on the bench became, the higher he foresaw his fine.

The chairperson banged her gavel once more. 'If there are any further interruptions, I shall clear the court.'

Both the magistrates and the usher glared across at Kelvin, ready to pounce should he open his mouth. It opened but only to let out a gasp as Ivor, sitting next to him, sank his elbow into his mid-riff. Kelvin disappeared from general view behind the leather jacket as he slid to the floor, fighting to get air into his lungs. Ivor put his boot on the back of his neck in order to keep him there for the time being, receiving a look of gratitude from the usher who was in a position to see what he was doing.

The business of the court finally got under way. There were a couple of poachers, both of whom received jail sentences. There was a wife beater who was fined £25 and, judging by the look he gave his missus as he left the dock, he was likely to be making a repeat appearance before too long. A couple of young men were up for pushing broken bottles in each other's face at a disco and they were put into the care of the leather jacket who turned out to be a probation officer. The greatest degree of calumny was reserved for a farmer who diverted a stream through his slurry pit when it needed emptying, and it was his bad luck that he should have been on the receiving end of the chairperson's election address before she fined him £200.

Then came the TV-licence offenders. The commander had slid forward several rows during the breaks between cases and was now well away from Kelvin who had become sulkily silent since Ivor had released him. Consequently only the squire knew of his connection to the earlier disturbances and the squire had been shooting poisonous glances at him and us throughout the morning. The commander, to the bafflement of Mr Harbottle and a solicitor from the Post Office, was the only accused who had turned up to plead not guilty. The rest were represented by a pile of cringing letters, all pleading guilty. The commander was summoned to the dock. He looked extremely impressive – upstanding, white-moustached, besuited and sober – and the chairperson looked benevolently upon his countenance. The old magistrate had dropped a box of paper handkerchiefs on the floor during the chairperson's peroration on the evils of modern agriculture and he appeared to have lost interest in his duties as he scrabbled around trying to recover them. The squire was still in a foul mood. He leaned over and whispered something in the chairperson's ear. She spoke to the commander.

'My colleague has indicated that he knows this defendant and is prepared to step down. Have you any objection to his remaining on the bench?'

The commander considered. It was a tricky decision. Having a friend at court should have been a highly desirable state of affairs but the squire was not in a state of mind in which it would be wise to depend on his benevolence.

'Well?' prompted the chairperson.

'I have no objection, M'Lud.'

The squire snorted in derision, but the chairperson almost simpered. 'It should be "Your Worship". I could feel that "M'Lud" was a little rude. It might at least have been "My Lady".'

Mr Harbottle of the Post Office was looking a bit concerned at this exchange, but the commander scented that he might be on to a good thing. He actually preened his moustache. 'My dear Madam Chairman, or should I say Chairlady, I can assure you that I used the title merely out of respect for your position and abilities. I would not dare to say in open court what my heart tells me that I would like to call you.'

'Jesus wept!' muttered Ivor into the startled silence, broken only by some semi-stifled giggles from the press bench.

The chairperson tittered. 'How very sweet of you—' The squire's snort brought back her sense of occasion. She reluctantly tore her eyes away from the commander. 'Er . . . Mr Macluckie.'

Mr Macluckie was the solicitor for the Post Office. He outlined the damning facts: how the commander had been caught watching television and how, eventually, he had been forced to admit that he had no licence. Mr Harbottle then came to the stand and corroborated all the evidence with the addition that the commander had originally claimed to have a licence. The squire frowned down at such perfidy and even the chairperson looked disapproving. The commander twizzled his moustache to keep his spirits up and refused to take advantage of the opportunity to question the witness. Mr Harbottle sat down and Mr Macluckie summed up the case for the prosecution and sat down with the air of a busy man who did not like to have to waste his time with idiots who defended the indefensible.

The usher addressed the commander. 'You may go into the

witness box and allow yourself to be cross-examined, or you may make a sworn statement from the witness box which would carry less weight, or you may speak from where you are which will carry least weight of all. Which do you wish to do?'

The commander looked vaguely round. 'I think I might as well stay where I am. It looks perfectly all right.'

'Very well. You may say what you wish.'

The commander put his hand in his pocket and fumbled round.

'Ah!' he said, pulling out his TV licence. 'Here we are. That fellow [indicating Mr Harbottle] said I hadn't got a licence. But I've got one here.'

There was a slight frisson from the Post Office. The chairperson leaned forward. 'You are not charged with not having a licence, Commander, but for not having a licence on 14 May.'

This was the commander's moment. 'With the greatest possible respect, Your Worships, it states on my indictment that I have been summonsed for not having a licence last week. It says nothing about 14 May.'

Consternation! Everyone examined their papers and the Post Office went into a huddle while the bench sent for and examined the commander's licence. The chairperson had the suspicion of a smile on her lips, but the squire did not appear to be amused. The old man was still retrieving tissues and had a respectable pile of them on his lap.

Mr Macluckie jumped to his feet. 'Your Worships, it appears that there may have been a clerical error, I would be grateful if you would allow us to correct it.'

'I'm very sorry, Mr Macluckie, but I'm afraid that you should have asked to change the date before the case was heard. You are too late now.'

'In that case, may we issue a fresh summons?'

There was a whispered discussion between the chairperson and the squire. It was closer to an argument and it was clear to those waiting for the result that the squire was losing, particularly after the chairperson had dug the old man in the ribs and startled him into an animated series of nods which went on like those of a toy dog in the back window of a car. She made her pronouncement. 'The defendant is found to be not guilty and he cannot be tried twice for the same offence, Mr Macluckie.'

And that was that.

The commander threw a celebration party a couple of nights later. He had been expecting to be found guilty and fined, so had cut down on his drinking and sold a consignment of radishes in order to amass £100 to go towards it. The money was aching to be squandered. Elfrieda wanted to donate the money to *Spare Rib* but the commander won through without too much diffiulty as she was quite fond of a party as well. They placed the television, in whose honour the party was being held, in the centre of the living room, surrounding it with chairs and arranged for the antiquated record player to have a good supply of Gilbert and Sullivan while a couple of barrels of beer were brought in from the pub. The commander declared open house and all flocked to do him homage. Even Kelvin said he had thought all along that he deserved to get off.

It was not a bad party. Mandy came down from her bijou cottage further up the village, having decked out her husband Keith for the occasion in a neat two-piece suit which contrasted ill with the professional drinking sweaters of everyone else. She took him back home early, however, which allowed him to return *sans* jacket after she had gone to bed. He was supposed to be working on the 'painting by numbers' portrait of a kitten that Mandy wished to give their teenage son for his birthday – she had refused his request for a year's subscription to *Mayfair*.

The squire turned up late and left early. Judging by his behaviour when he was there, it was hard to understand why he had bothered to come at all. He may have thought it his duty. He greeted Elfrieda and wandered over to the alcohol.

'Pretty disgraceful business that, Commander,' was his initial gambit as he watched his host milk a barrel on his behalf.

'You mean the way Kelvin behaved? Yes, I'm sorry about that. You must have found it embarrassing. I know I did.'

'I didn't just mean that. I've never believed that nonsense about better a hundred guilty going free rather than one innocent being punished, or whatever it is. I thought you deserved a bloody great fine and I hope you don't mind me saying so to your face.' The commander turned rather red about the gills as the squire continued, 'Mind you, even if you did mind me saying so, I'd still say it. I don't expect gentlemen to come before the court for that sort of thing. Lied to that little man from the Post Office too, didn't you? Friend of mine was once up for shooting a poacher. That's the sort of thing a chap could understand.'

The commander was doubly annoyed because he could see the truth in what the squire was saying. 'Look, I was charged with an offence and found not guilty.'

'Oh, quite. But both you and I know you didn't deserve to get off. Barrack-room lawyer's trick. It was that stupid woman who let you get away with it. I feel it's up to people of our kind to set an example to everyone else and we deserve to be heavily penalized when we don't. Wouldn't you agree?'

'No,' said the commander. 'I think everyone should be equal in the eyes of the law.'

'I still think you ought to be ashamed of yourself, letting the side down and all that.'

'Look, you don't have to come here to drink my beer and insult me.'

'I don't mean to be offensive. But you'd better make jolly sure that you aren't up before me again for stealing from the collection plate or anything. I'd make sure you wouldn't get away with it again. The law's not to be mocked with impunity, you know.'

'If there are people like you to administer it, how is it possible not to mock it?' snapped the commander.

This discussion had attracted an interested circle of spectators who were feeding on the raw emotions on display. The commander had been known to get cross before but it was rare to see the squire bandying insults. He had been known to

go around kicking disobedient gun dogs and there were certain words like 'Scargill' and 'Benn' that were always guaranteed to produce an interesting reaction but, to the villagers, he was normally the epitome of old-fashioned courtesy. It was not part of his code to argue in front of his social inferiors. He was not a snob, but he would normally no more behave like this than he would say 'dog' rather than 'hound'. His gout had much to answer for.

Ivor, ever the diplomat, stepped in. 'Shall we change the subject? It's all over, after all.'

'As long as I receive an apology,' said the commander stiffly.

'I'm damned if you'll get an apology from me, I'm only sorry we had this conversation in your own house. If you'll excuse me.' The squire turned round and left the room.

There was a buzz of interested conversation after he had left. Many had been disappointed that the commander had not been found guilty, but this was almost as good.

Ten minutes later, to everyone's surprise, the squire returned, looking even more agitated than when he had gone out.

'What do you want?' said the commander.

'It's my car. I can't get it going.'

'What a shame! You can always walk home. It won't take you more than fifteen minutes.'

'Look, I'm sorry about what I said earlier on. I take it back. I wouldn't really have wanted to see you go to jail.'

'That's nice to know anyway. What do you want? A push? Or a lift?'

'I'm blocking the entrance to your yard, I'm afraid. I don't think anyone else can get out.'

'Let's go and have a look.'

Many of the guests followed them out. Before the commander and Elfrieda had bought their house, it had been owned by a retired farmer from 'up country' – in his case it meant from the flat cornlands about 20 miles east. He had made sufficient of a pile when he sold his farm to have had delusions of gentility and had converted the barns into up-to-date stables to house his hunters and had concreted the old yard. The yard was currently used to store the dismantled greenhouses and sheds that the commander found irresistible at sales. At its exit on to the road, two tall pillars had been erected, each capped by a stone ball about a foot in diameter. The squire, for some obscure reason, had decided to reverse out of the yard and, his vision obscured by a dog grille to which were clipped gun racks, had failed to negotiate the narrow space between the two pillars. He had brushed the left-hand one and brought down the stone ball on to the bonnet of his estate car.

'Oh dear,' said Ivor. 'How on earth did you manage that?'

'I don't quite know. I wasn't really concentrating and sort of went squint. The car won't start. I think it's quite serious.'

'Ho-ho,' said the commander.

'Ha-ha,' agreed Elfrieda, who had not appreciated the squire's handling of her mate.

'It's not a joke,' said the squire.

'Tee-hee,' said the commander, pulling out a handkerchief and wiping tears from his eyes.

'Honestly!' said the squire.

The commander was in no condition to be useful and he went back into the house to recover from what was beginning to look dangerously like hysteria. Kelvin and several others heaved the bits of ball off the car and put them out of the way, returning to inspect the damage. With some difficulty the buckled bonnet was prised open and a torch was found in order to examine the interior.

'It's smashed your distributor,' said Ivor. 'You won't be going anywhere until you get another cap for it. The bonnet's not in too great shape either.'

'I'm perfectly capable of seeing that!' snapped the squire. 'I only just touched that pillar. That damn ball must have been just balancing on top, waiting for any breeze to come along and blow it off. Criminally negligent to have something in that condition. Someone could easily have been killed.'

Kelvin stiffened in excitement. 'Criminally negligent, squire? That sounds as though it might be against the law.'

'Oh, do shut up, Kelvin!' said Lindy. 'We've had enough trouble for one night.'

'It's our duty to uphold the law,' said Kelvin virtuously.

'You're absolutely right, Kelvin. I've a damn good mind to report it to the police,' said the squire.

'I'm sure Percy would take it very seriously. Criminal negligence and all that. Especially with you being a magistrate. You might even end up trying the case.'

'So I might,' said the squire brightening.

'Why not let's push your car out of the way and come in and have another drink, Squire. I can run you home later,' said Ivor.

'That could be construed wrongly, you know,' said Kelvin. 'Taking favours from accused persons. That was the beginning of the end for Bobby Moore, you know.'

'What *are* you talking about?' asked Ivor.

'It was Bobby Moore, wasn't it? That bloke who had his head chopped off in a film on telly the other night?'

'Sir Thomas More, you mean.'

'That's the bloke. Anyway, he first got into trouble for accepting a cup from a woman who was supposed to be coming up before him.'

'That's quite true,' said the squire. 'I saw that film too. Perhaps I ought to leave now.'

Lindy had had enough of this. 'Kelvin, do shut up. You're just trying to make trouble.'

'It's nothing to do with you, Lindy,' said Kelvin.

Lindy turned to Ivor. 'Do you know whereabouts Kelvin had a carbuncle a few months back?'

Before Ivor had time to translate the gleam of interest in his eyes into words, Kelvin broke in. 'All right, all right. I'll hold my peace.'

'Thank you, Kelvin,' she replied sweetly. She took control and ordered the voyeurs to push the car out of the way before ushering the squire back into the party. She then led him over to the commander. 'It's time you two made up,' she said briskly.

The commander had regained control of himself. He had

enjoyed the sight of the squashed motor car so much that he was quite happy to make friends again. Lindy left them to it, which was a pity as it gave Kelvin the opportunity to play Iago once more.

'Hope you didn't take offence, Commander,' said the squire a little stiffly.

'Not at all. Elfrieda has moods like this sometimes. She calls it pre-menstrual tension. Come to think on it, she's been much better lately.'

'Something to do with being over fifty, dear. You're a bit of a freak if you have PMT at my age,' said Elfrieda.

'I can assure you that I do not suffer from PMT,' said the squire, who did not know what it was but suspected that it was something female and terrible. 'My gout has been playing up a bit. Marcia says I'm hell to live with.'

Kelvin was hovering at the squire's elbow. 'Aye, it's a terrible thing, gout. Adam Pennyfeather, he that died forty years ago, used to suffer from gout. Said it was like having a carthorse standing on his toe. He was a drunkard, of course.'

One was never quite sure whether or not there was a *double entendre* in many of Kelvin's utterances. Ivor played the accordion which Kelvin had once described, with wistful sincerity, as being as beautiful as the sound of a litter of new-born piglets. The squire remained silent while he tried to work out if he had just been insulted, so Kelvin continued to make innocent conversation. 'You were lucky out there, Commander. The squire reckons he could have had you for having that there stone in a dangerous condition.'

'What do you mean?' asked the commander.

'Criminal negligence, that's what he reckoned it was.'

'Really? Well at least you were wise enough not to make a fool of yourself on that one, Squire.'

'Quite,' said the squire.

'Fool of himself?' said Kelvin, working away busily. 'If what the squire says is right, that stone was just hanging there by a thread, waiting to crush some kiddie walking past.'

'Balls!' scoffed the commander. 'It took a bloody great

Volvo ramming into it, driven by a fool who wasn't looking where he was going to bring it down.'

Kelvin sighed with pleasure.

'Good God, you're a shit, Kelvin,' said Elfrieda.

'I'm not a fool. Nor did I ram the pillar. I merely scraped it,' said the squire testily.

'Of course, of course. A couple of hundredweight of solid rock cemented into a saucer leapt like a fairy on to your car when it saw you coming.' The commander had begun to chortle again.

The squire, to the satisfaction of Kelvin, was reddening up. 'I said it then and I'll say it again now. It was criminal negligence. If I took the matter any further, you wouldn't worm your way out of it a second time.' He waggled his finger under the commander's nose. 'Oh no you wouldn't. I'd make jolly sure that there were no slip-ups this time. The least I intend to do is sue you for the damage you did to my motor car. You'll be hearing from my solicitors. Kelvin, I'd be grateful if you could take me home now.'

'Hang on, Squire. The party's not over. There's plenty of beer left in the barrel.' But he was speaking to the squire's fast-disappearing back. In the latter's childhood, underlings had always done as he asked and he had not quite grown out of the habit of expecting it always to be so. 'Oh hell, I suppose I'd better take the silly old bugger home.'

The commander looked after them with narrowed eyes. Elfrieda glanced at him with concern. 'Oh dear,' she said, 'I haven't seen anyone look so cross since I pinched a policeman's bottom up at Greenham.'

The commander poured some more beer, forgot the squire and got on with the party.

The manor was little more than half a mile away from the commander's farm. Neither household was particularly quick off the mark, but their opening salvos would have crossed each other on their way to their respective targets. The squire used more sophisticated weaponry. Through the commander's letterbox came a letter from a firm of London solicitors which informed him that their client intended to sue for damage to his motor car caused by the commander's negligence unless reparation for the damage was speedily made.

The commander was more direct. He had merely sent the squire a postcard telling him that, since he had broken the stone ball, he was expected to replace it. There was a quote of £175 for the manufacture and installation of a suitable ball which was available for inspection. The commander felt himself so secure in his position that he did not react with the outrage that might have been expected to the communication from the squire's legal advisers. He took a postcard from Elfrieda's desk with a large CND symbol on the front, which he knew would annoy, and sent it to the squire. He pointed out that nobody else over the three years he had been in the village had hit the post, that he could produce witnesses who could say that the squire had been drinking and who had heard him say that he was not paying attention when he had bashed into the pillar and that he, the commander, would start getting nasty unless his stone was replaced forthwith. It produced the desired reaction.

Postcards through the mail served a specific purpose in the community. They were used to mobilize public opinion on the sender's behalf. Ordinary complaints and gossip were overt but both Maud and Father Loosemire, the postie, read the messages on the cards and the information they gleaned from them had more impact since it was supposed to be confidential. When one used a postcard, one always had to be aware of one's wider public – a bit like a cabinet minister writing his private diaries. The commander's postcard yielded a more direct benefit. Father Loosemire told his son Jason about it; Jason was currently supplementing his social security payments by working as a builder and went straight round to see the squire with the upshot that he arrived on the commander's doorstep the following day.

The commander was a Wodehouse fan and he called his pig the Empress after that owned by Lord Emsworth. He also liked to contemplate it and scratch it. He had recently discovered that, if he scratched its belly rather than its back, the pig would stop whatever it was doing and fall on its side, grunting with delight. This gave him a feeling of great power as well as exciting his scientific curiosity. He had succeeded in making the Empress lie down in a bed of nettles and in a bramble bush and he was working on his latest experiment. He was absorbed in carefully placing some pigmeal on a small patch of concrete which had been sown with broken bricks. Jason came, stood and pondered.

'Afternoon, Commander,' he said eventually.

The commander had been so interested in his task that he had not noticed Jason's approach. Jason had been stealing pheasants for fifteen of his twenty years and stealthy movements had become second nature. The commander jumped. 'Oh, hullo. I didn't see you coming.' He looked a little guilty.

'If you don't mind me asking, what exactly are you doing?' queried Jason.

'We . . . I'm carrying out an experiment.'

'Oh, I see. An experiment.' Jason was an old-fashioned country lad in that he had truanted all his school days and was scarcely literate. Experiments were things that educated people did, like reading books and keeping money in banks instead of in the tea caddy. All such behaviour was incomprehensible and therefore not worth bothering with. 'I've been told by the squire to replace your stone ball.'

'Really?' The commander was a bit annoyed. 'He might have bloody well told me that he was admitting liability.'

'I don't know about that, but it means he admits it was his fault. I'm to send my bill to him.'

'I'm glad to hear it. But I think it would have been better if he had let me organize the repair and sent the bill on to him afterwards. I've had somebody quote already and I would have liked to have chosen him to do the job.'

'Yeah, I thought you might, so I went to the squire and offered to do it for £150. If you don't make waves, there's £50 in it for you.'

'How dare you!' exclaimed the commander, his honour impugned.

'All right, I'll make it £60, if you sign my bill to say you're satisfied with the job.'

'£60! How on earth can you afford to give me £60 out of it?'

Jason shuffled in apparent embarrassment. 'You won't tell, will you?'

'Tell what?'

'Tell what I'm going to tell you.'

The commander worked it out after a few seconds' pause. 'No, all right. I promise not to tell.'

Jason looked smug. 'I know where there's the spitting image of that ball and I reckon I can get hold of it.'

'You're not suggesting that you're going to steal someone else's ball?'

'Did I say that?' demanded Jason, trying to look offended. 'Don't worry, it'll never be missed.'

'I certainly do not intend to condone theft.'

'There's £60 in it. All you've got to do is sign the bill. I'll say on it that I made the bloody ball myself and that'll let everyone off the hook if there's any comeback.'

'I know absolutely nothing about it,' said the commander.

' 'Course you don't,' replied Jason encouragingly.

The commander stood up and squared his shoulders. 'Right. Just so long as that's understood. When will you finish?'

'It's already done, my son.' Jason liked to watch television programmes like *Minder* and *The Professionals*. 'I've just finished.'

'You might have bloody well checked with me first.'

'You weren't around.'

'Yes I was. I was out here. It can't have taken long.'

'It didn't. I had the ball already, you see. Come and have a look and then you can sign that I've done it and we can get our money off the squire.'

'Even if I do get £60, I'm not signing anything unless it's a good job,' warned the commander as he followed Jason round the side of the house.

They crossed the courtyard and halted beneath the pillar and the commander looked up and scrutinized the ball.

'See?' said Jason. 'It's a bloody fine bit of work. It matches the other ball perfectly.'

The commander was grudgingly forced to agree. 'Hmm. It's not bad. The colour's a bit funny.'

'A month or two of weather will soon put that right. I've got the bill here. Will you sign?'

'I suppose so.' The commander got out his reading glasses and carefully perused the document. It needed careful perusal since Jason had been its author. 'Loosemire has only one "m",' said the commander, mentioning the most important flaw that he could see. He took the proffered pen from Jason and signed as instructed, adding 'in full and final settlement'. 'Thank you very much, Jason.'

'Quite all right, Commander. I'll get your money to you just as soon as the squire settles.'

Jason paid his money and, as the squire's gout improved, he and the commander made friends once again. It would have been the end of the matter, too, had not the pigeons decided to move into the commander's lettuces. He bought a .22 air rifle and spent all hours of the day in makeshift hides waiting to ambush them as they arrived to steal his produce. The birds obviously thought him some kind of nut and found it safer to move in after he had retired to the house for his meals, having first disentangled himself from his camouflage of strawberry netting intertwined with grass.

Then one morning he was awakened by one of the offending birds cooing at him. He crawled to his bedroom window with his air rifle and, ignoring Elfrieda's protests, slid open the sash and shot at it. There were several things that did not work out as the commander intended. First of all, his target was a perfectly innocuous collared dove. That did not matter too much, since the commander missed it. What was unfortunate was that the bird had been cooing from the new ball. The commander's shot struck this perch fair and square and, to the palpitating horror of both the bird and the commander, the ball exploded with a loud report and sagged down on the top of the pillar.

The squire found it all a great joke. The commander had

signed the bill for the replacement of the damaged ball and it was his own fault if he had failed to observe that Jason had stuck up a plastic football that he had painted grey. The commander recalled his £60 and how he had been led to believe that he was profiting from stolen goods, and swallowed his indignation as best he could. Jason himself was unavailable for comment since he was in police custody answering questions on sheep rustling. The squire dismissed the charge the following week. They had been very small sheep, he explained to the surprised court, and there had not been very many of them.

Chapter Eight

ALTHOUGH THE manor was still there, gently decaying through successive centuries of summer heat and winter frost, it was no longer the economic powerhouse of the parish. The days when most of the village depended for its living on the largesse that emanated from the capricious and bottomless pockets of the big house, in domestic service, as tradesmen and as workers on the land supplying its various needs, had vanished. The cunning which had enabled the squire's ancestors to back the right side in 1688 and thus establish a dynasty, had been bred out of his descendants over the years. While the ancestral brains had been lost, the ancestral beauty had remained until the Great War which had enabled the amiable grand- and great-grandfathers of the current squire to ensnare heiresses and keep them in the manner to which they had grown accustomed, but even this talent had disappeared with the squire's father. He had married the daughter of a bishop, a financial disaster, and his son, the present incumbent, had also married for love.

Now the squire had only the mouldering manor and a few hundred acres of wood and scrub in place of the few thousand that he had inherited. Several of the canny yokels whose ancestors had depended on the manor for their existence could now have bought him out, but the villagers preserved the fiction that the manor was the fountainhead of the community. The squire was still the monarch, albeit the constitutional monarch, of the horticultural society, the parochial church council and the committee which, for twelve years, had been trying to raise the funds necessary to build a village hall.

The squire and his wife had four children. The eldest worked for a merchant bank in London, another was in the army, the third had married a farm in Gloucestershire, showing that not all the ancestral skills had been dissipated, and the fourth was a daughter called Caroline. She had attended the village primary school before being packed off to Benenden, from where she had returned during the holidays to ride furiously in gymkhanas and learn the simplistic ways of rural love from some of the lusty local youths. She passed on this knowledge to a whole generation of stammering graduates of *Penthouse* and single-sex public schools on the county circuit of hunt balls when she would lead them out into the rose garden to taste wonders that they had only dreamed about. Many dim, horsy wives later had reason to thank her, but they never knew it.

Caroline was a lovely, warm-hearted girl and the village was sorry to lose her when she found a job with a little art gallery just off Bond Street. But her mother proudly showed her photograph round the village when she appeared in glossy magazines as a guest at a wedding, talking to dukes and earls or at the grand London charity balls. She still sometimes came down to the village at weekends and gently rebuffed those of her old friends, most now laden with the responsibilities of wives, small children and the need to pay the rent, who considered that their early tuition in the art of love had left them with life-long rights to give her revision.

Then her photograph appeared as the frontispiece of *Country Life*. Caroline was engaged to the heir of a bart. He was not only the heir of a bart, according to the squire's wife, but he was loaded as well: oodles of boodle which manifested itself in Porsches, helicopter trips, fast motorbikes and a pop group all of his own, with himself on drums, which played at smart dances within a hundred-mile radius of London and turned out records which were bought by all his friends and were played at the fashionable discotheques.

The quality of being extraordinarily rich is still surprisingly common among the British aristocracy. What is much rarer is the ability to spend it with enjoyment. The aristocracy have been cowed by a century of terror of the fiscal tumbrils and by the concept of *noblesse* having to *oblige*. Few are aware that the great mass of the proletariat could no longer care less about them and that there is nothing, save their own lack of imagination, to prevent them coming out of the financial closet to join the pop stars and vulgarly successful entrepreneurs.

The wedding was to be an extravaganza. There was a problem with the size of the village church into which it was impossible to shoehorn more than a couple of hundred people. This did not matter at the funerals of some of the old hunting farmers which always had a good turn-out. The service, conducted by the frozen-faced anti-bloodsports vicar inside the church, was a far less successful and appropriate affair than the alternative mourning amongst the gravestones in the churchyard outside where his cronies sat and pulled on their whisky flasks while discussing the antics of the departed on the hunting field. For the wedding, it was decided that the church should be filled by the country grandees in their Edwardian morning suits redolent with the odour of mothballs which would be exhumed for the occasion, whilst the godless metropolitan social butterflies, amid whom the happy couple had passed the previous few years, would have to be content with attending the reception which was to be held in a huge marquee on the manor lawn.

It was looked forward to as the largest and most spectacular social event held in the village for the past half-century, particularly when it was learned that a brace of minor royals had been invited. This was discovered by Maud at the post office who had vetted the addresses on the envelopes after the squire's wife had put the invitations into the pillar box. There was a careful social gradation at functions like this. People like Ivor and Dennis who farmed and spoke proper were invited. The commander spoke proper and sort of farmed, but he had not been in the village long enough to be asked. Others, such as Kelvin and Bill farmed, much more successfully than the squire, Ivor or Dennis but, although they could trace their local ancestry back through the centuries and into the Tudor mists, they spoke with the local accent and would not expect to be asked.

Originally the social divide had been a matter of class; now it was cultural. None of those not on the invitation list, save possibly the commander who had been trained to prostrate himself before more senior officers, considered those invited of higher class than themselves. But they no more expected to be asked than they would expect the squire to come to a whist drive in aid of the skittle team or turn up in the room behind the pub where, on a Saturday night, an organist played such ditties as *Home Sweet Home* and *Widecombe Fair* for everyone to join in. In the same way a maharajah might have met a duke: both men might like each other and respect each other but neither really envied the other. Deep down they both knew that the other was their inferior and could hardly be expected to observe their shibboleths.

As the wedding grew closer, it began to generate business. Because of the distance from 'town', guests were quartered in country houses for miles around, but a gaggle of what Caroline referred to as 'Hooray Henrys', who included the best man and the ushers, were booked into the fishing hotel that lay a mile or so downstream of the village. Mick was asked to tender for the supply of champagne and Caroline neatly press-ganged many of her old swains into acting as waiters and ferried them all in to the nearest dress-hire shop so that they could all be kitted out. Percy, the local policeman, became insufferably self-important. He was in charge of security for the royals. He had not actually been officially notified as to their attendance, but Maud had carefully checked the replies to the invitations, had asked the squire's wife about the one with the pretty coat of arms on the back of the envelope and passed the resultant information on to Percy and everyone else who came into the post office.

One way and another, a substantial proportion of the villagers were involved in the wedding; those who were not included the hard core of people who spent most of their time in the pub. But they did not want to be left out entirely. The knowledge that there were Hooray Henrys to be found in the hotel the night before the festivities gave them sufficient incentive to leave their regular habitat to go down to take in a slice of the action there. The regulars were not entirely sure what a Hooray Henry was and were most interested in finding out. Bernard, the new vet, came along, as well as Dennis – Bernard because he had very nearly become a Hooray Henry himself, and Dennis because he suspected that he may well have been one during his youth. They were to be our experts in case there was difficulty with identification.

Although the hotel lay only just beyond the parish boundary, it had nothing in common with the village or its way of life. It was a great, grey Victorian structure, inside which time did not appear to have moved since the 1930s. Immense stuffed trout, the like of which had not been seen in the river in living memory, clung to the walls between hunting prints and gloomy oil paintings of highland cattle hunching themselves to withstand the onslaught of rainstorms sweeping down the side of the mountain to overwhelm the glen in which they stand. Most of the furniture was antique and the tables in the lounge were scattered with issues of the *Field* and old bound copies of *Punch*. The clientele matched. It is said that one can go into any country pub and shout 'Major' and someone will answer. But this was not a pub, it was a sporting hotel, and here one could shout 'General' or 'Admiral' and be sure that some bent old man would turn his frosty eye towards you to check whether you wanted him or the other general at the next table.

During the day these ancient warriors would spread themselves along the various beats of the river which were owned by the hotel, cast a few shaky flies at the water and then retire to the shade of the conveniently placed willows along the bank to sup their flasks of whisky well out of the way of their wives who stayed behind to gossip about who did what to whom in Gib. or Ootacamund in 1932. In the evening they tottered home with, if they were lucky, a couple of sardine-sized trout apiece, for dinner, more whisky and bed.

The establishment was presided over by Julian Shaw, an exceedingly precious ex-interior decorator who had inherited it from an aunt. He was a very good host to his own specialized type of guest. He called the warhorses 'Sir' and flirted with their wives who were all old enough to describe him as 'such a gay young man' without the thought of a *double entendre* in their heads.

The hotel had a slightly uneasy relationship with the village. Julian was an entirely urban animal who played a part very successfully to woo his guests, but he found it hard to cope with raw rurality. The sight of an early-morning rabbit defecating on the immaculate lawn that lay in front of the hotel made him shudder with disgust and he had had to leave a pre-Christmas drinks party given by Ivor shortly after he had taken over the hotel when Kelvin had held the rest of us spellbound with his description of a particularly difficult calving of a couple of twins which had called for mouth-to-

mouth resuscitation. Although Julian was invariably polite to the locals, he did not put himself out to make them welcome. His aunt had tolerated a crude, sawdust-carpeted public bar behind the hotel, known as 'the Snuggery', which was reached by going past the dustbins and through a small alley that throbbed in unison with the ancient coal-fired central-heating boiler, but Julian had closed it down and now used it as an annex to house young men who were there to learn the hotelier's profession. It had now been re-christened 'the Buggery', which may or may not have been unfair.

Julian was understandably rather alarmed to see a group of yokels come steaming in to the lobby of the hotel and pause, looking hopefully round them. He abandoned a querulous old dowager who was complaining at the reception desk about the temperature of her hot-water bottle when she woke up in the early hours of the morning and failed to get back to sleep.

'Er . . . hullo, Kelvin, Commander. What can I do for you?'

'Hello, young Julian,' replied Kelvin. 'We just thought it was time that we had a drink in your lounge bar for a change. We can't show favouritism, you know, and someone pointed out that we give too much of our custom to the pub in the village and that we ought to spread our money around a bit.'

The others glanced at Kelvin with approval. Julian's opinion of the rough trade was well known, but it would have been difficult to react churlishly and kick out someone who had his interests so clearly at heart. Julian himself looked as if he might be tempted to try the difficult thing but Kelvin flashed the best that he could muster in the way of a friendly grin. This consisted of parting his lips to display his false teeth. Kelvin's bottom plate was anchored to the blackened remnants of his own teeth which stood out like the spars of an ancient wreck from a sand bar. Julian reared away in alarm, but Kelvin was used to this type of reaction to his friendly grins and, no doubt, interpreted it as a start of delight.

'Er . . .' faltered Julian, his winsome charm momentarily deserting him.

'Young man!' boomed the dowager by the desk impatiently.

Julian rolled his eyes unto the wood-panelled ceiling and

returned to the reception desk. Kelvin and the rest of us clumped across the worn Persian carpets into the bar, our antennae twitching for any evidence of a Hooray Henry.

There was one other guest present, an old man crooning over a large gin and a springer spaniel that lay at his feet. Judging by the immensity of his white handlebar moustache, he was a retired air-marshal. Behind the bar was Patrick, one of the many youngish men in the parish who did a bit of this and a bit of that in order to earn a crust. They would do anything as long as it did not interfere with their hunting and as long as it came in cash so that it would not jeopardize their social security payments. Like almost everyone in the area, he was related to both Kelvin and Bill and stopped reading the racing pages of his paper to greet us warmly.

'Get your dirty paws out of there!' he said as Kelvin and Bill stuck their fists straight into the two bowls of peanuts that lay on the bar, removing half the contents of each. 'Does Mr Shaw know you're here? We're expecting to be rather busy later on.'

'I know,' said Kelvin. 'That's *why* we're here.'

Before Patrick could pursue that fox, the door to the bar opened and a couple of tall men in their twenties wearing dinner jackets came in. They looked rather alike, although one had dark hair and the other had blond.

Kelvin stiffened. 'Are those Hooray Henrys?' he asked in a hoarse whisper.

Dennis looked them carefully over. 'They could well be,' he admitted, as they came up to the bar alongside us and stood politely as Patrick filled our order. Kelvin and Bill examined them critically and openly. It takes a great deal to pierce the skin of a Hooray Henry and make him uncomfortable but the combined stare of those two would have wiped the smile off the face of the Mona Lisa and made her wonder if her slip might be showing. The Henrys began to shoot nervous glances at their neighbours. One of them – the dark one – smiled placatingly.

'Good evening,' he said. His smile was very sweet.

'Christ!' breathed Kelvin, a man unused to the social graces, 'I think the man's a bloody poofter like Julian.'

The commander frowned at Kelvin to shut him up. 'Good evening. Lovely weather we're having, isn't it?'

'Yes. Jolly hot. Could do with a spot of rain.'

'What the hell are those two going on about the weather for?' whispered Kelvin to Dennis.

'They're being polite. Good manners are the oil of social intercourse.'

'Not in public, I hope. I never knew that Hooray Henrys did that sort of thing,' said Kelvin.

'I'm not sure that I quite understand,' said Dennis puzzled.

'Social intercourse,' muttered Kelvin darkly from behind the hand that he was holding over his mouth so that he could not be overheard by anyone less than half a mile away.

The Hooray Henry, if that's what he was, and the commander were still labouring away trying to ignore the ripples among the rest of the bar customers that their innocuous little conversation was creating. It was difficult, and the blond one turned directly to Bill.

'Pretty country round here, don't you think?' he said.

Bill did not think it was pretty. He had lived in it all his life and it was just home but, for politeness's sake, he was willing to grapple with this unusual concept.

'Some of it, I suppose. A lot of the moorland is rubbish but there are one or two decent farms. Is your name Henry?'

'No. Roy, actually.'

'Are you here for the wedding?'

'Yes. Do you know Caroline's parents?'

' 'Course I do. He's the squire, isn't he? Patrick here knew Caroline well, once upon a time. He's my wife's cousin's son. Where do you come from?'

One could see Roy delicately toying with the word 'knew', wondering if it could mean what he thought it could mean.

'Come from? Oh, we farm in Yorkshire.' If he had been brought up in the country, he probably knew about 'knowing'.

'Farm do you? What sort of farming?'

'A little bit of this and that. You know the sort of thing.'

'How many acres?'

'I think it's about 5000.' This brought about a startled

hush. Our region was too remote from the centres of power ever to have attracted the great magnates seeking to establish their dynasties by buying up vast tracts of the countryside. Our farmers were the yeomen of England, each with a hundred or so acres passed down through the generations and hardly a tenant amongst them. There was only one land owner within 50 miles who owned an estate of comparable size.

Kelvin was first to break the thoughtful silence. 'Do you do beef?'

'I think so.'

'I've got some really good pedigree Devons that I might be willing to sell.'

Bill nearly spat his beer out on to the bar. Kelvin *had* had some pedigree Devons which he had bought nearly ten years before, but their pedigree had been greatly diluted as a result of incursions by a randy little Hereford bull belonging to the dairy farmer next door. Roy, the dark Henry, was spared the necessity of responding to Kelvin's kind offer by the arrival of another half-dozen dinner-jacketed aristocrats. Patrick had topped up all our glasses, and so we retired to the far end to observe. There were lots of people living in the neighbourhood who had been born with plums in their mouths – with three thriving hunts within a dozen miles it was unavoidable – but this lot seemed to have spat out their plums and replaced them with melons. Another one came through the door and emitted a noise.

'What did he say?' whispered Bill to Kelvin.

'He said "Air, hair, lair," I think,' replied Kelvin, 'but I can't think why.' He nudged the commander. 'What's he talking about?'

'Shh,' said the commander. 'It's just the way he speaks. He said, "Oh, hullo." '

Kelvin was entranced. 'Go on,' he said incredulously. 'Did he really?'

'Yes, he really did.'

'Air, hair, lair. I must remember that.' Kelvin had rolling West Country 'rs' and it did not come out of his mouth with quite the same purity of diction as it had from the mouth of the Henry, but Kelvin loved it. He rumbled away contentedly, practising this new language, at idle moments during the rest of the evening.

The Henrys were not hanging about. When they went to the bar to order a whisky or a gin, it was not the normal gnat's pee-sized measure that was poured into their glasses, but Patrick handed full bottles across and he didn't even take any money for them. It was all put down on the slate. Over the course of the next hour, they became more and more loud and more and more melonic in their vowel sounds. The air-marshal eventually decided he had had enough. He rose to his feet, waited for a lull in their conversation, let out a snort of contempt that would have been appropriate from a shire mare being propositioned by a Shetland stallion and stalked out of the room, his spaniel skulking after him. The Henrys appeared oblivious, but we were nearer the door and we could hear him bollocking Julian who was at the reception desk outside. His voice was a growled protest while Julian could be heard verbally washing his hands like an obsequious Edwardian grocer's assistant. After pacifying the guest, Julian came through to the lounge bar to see what all the fuss was about. He looked distastefully at the group of locals, saucer-eyed at the amount of spirits that the Henrys were consuming and went up to Patrick.

'Have they got going yet?'

'I think they're just warming up, Julian.'

'I wish they'd bloody well get a move on. I'm going to start losing guests soon.'

'Get a move on doing what, Julian?' asked Kelvin with interest.

'Get a move on running up a decent bill,' replied Julian. There was a crash from the corner as one of the Henrys overbalanced on his chair and fell to the ground. 'Aha!' cried mine host and he rushed over, full of apologies, to help him back to an upright position. He returned to the bar. 'That's a bit more like it, Patrick. Stick down £20 damages.'

'But the chair's not broken.'

'That silly sod is too drunk to notice so shove it down.'

'You're running a bloody clip joint,' exclaimed the commander.

'You don't have to be here. In fact, I wouldn't object if you weren't here at all,' snapped Julian nastily.

'You watch your tongue, Julian,' warned Kelvin.

'In my own establishment, I can do precisely as I please.'

'And I own the field next door and I am about due to spread some chicken shit.' It was believed that the only reason that Kelvin still kept chickens was in order to be able to make this threat to people who displeased him.

'If you bloody well dared, Kelvin, I'd have the law on you.'

'A fat lot of good that would do you when Percy wants to do some pigeon shooting on my land this year,' countered Kelvin smugly.

One of the Henrys approached the bar, placing a tumblerful of whisky on its top. He was awfully polite and awfully drunk.

'Excuse me,' he said.

'Yes sir?' said Julian, wiping the frown from his face as he turned from Kelvin to a rich customer.

'I do hope you'll forgive me, but those glasses up there . . .' He paused.

'Which glasses?' asked Julian helpfully. The Henry was swaying on his feet, so Julian shooed the commander from his stool and placed it carefully beneath the Henry who subsided gratefully back on to it. He pointed his arm towards the ceiling.

'Those up there in that rack thing.' We followed his gesture.

'Above the bar!' exclaimed Kelvin in the tone of one who has just guessed the object in a difficult game of I-spy-with-my-little-eye.

'That's right!' said the Henry with delight. Along the full length of the bar were a couple of strips of wood between which was suspended a long line of wine glasses which were held there by their bases. We all looked at them.

'They're certainly very interesting,' said Julian politely. 'But what about them?'

The Henry stood up from his stool. 'I do hope you will forgive me, but this is something that I have always wanted to do.' He reached up to the glass at the far end and, with a look of solemn concentration on his face he took hold of its bowl and pushed it along the rack. The principle was much the same as that employed by engine drivers when they shunt wagons: the whole line of glasses moved along and one at the other end fell off. Bill, still retaining his stool, carefully moved it aside as the glasses began to patter down from the roof. Alerted by the sound, the air-marshal put his head round the door to investigate and stayed, spell-bound, to watch.

There must have been nearly a hundred glasses hanging from the rack and, to begin with, they did not give up their lives easily. As the Henry pushed, they grated together and overlapped at their bases. A couple even expired prematurely as their bowls shattered under the pressure imposed on them by their neighbours. By the time twenty per cent of them were on the floor, the line began to move faster and they plopped down from their launch points with a precision and regularity that would have inspired Isaac Newton to carve his niche in history decades before he did, had he not been forced to wait for the revelation beneath his apple tree.

For those of us who would not be involved in clearing up the mess or having to make good this glassy genocide, it was a deeply moving experience. As the majestic procession continued to shuffle along the rack to cascade to its destruction in a glitter of climactic splinters, the Henry's audience was entranced. So was the Henry. There was a dreamy look on his face as if he were listening to the orchestra starting up for the opening dance at his very first Queen Charlotte's Ball.

The last glass toppled lazily down from the rack and the Henry took down his arm, carefully picked up his whisky and took a small sip. There was complete silence in the room although, from the lobby behind the air-marshal, whose red face and bulging eyeballs spoke of an unquiet spirit within, there were hoots and nasal brays as the gerontocracy of the British armed forces sought to establish whether the sound of all that breaking glass meant that the enemy were coming through the windows at them.

Kelvin was first to break the hallowed silence. 'By heck. That was lovely. You know what that reminded me of? It was like when you go into a well-cropped sheep pasture in the autumn with your plough and it cuts its way neatly through the turf. There's something so right about it.'

'Or the look of an even bunch of store cattle,' Bill contributed.

'Or cleanly killing a really difficult pheasant,' said Dennis. 'It's the simple pleasure of seeing a job well done.'

The Henry was coming out of his trance. He reached inside

his pocket and brought out a cheque book, looking at Julian. 'How much do I owe you?'

Julian looked gloomily down at the wreckage. 'It'll take some clearing up and there must have been not far short of a hundred glasses there. They alone must have been worth £50.'

'Bring me a dustpan and a brush and I'll clear it up,' said Kelvin. 'It doesn't seem fair that you should be the only one to pay, because we all enjoyed it.'

'That's awfully kind of you,' said the Henry, looking enormously gratified.

'Think nothing of it,' replied Kelvin, crunching across the glass shards on the carpet and putting his arm round the Henry's shoulder. 'Do you often do things in that sort of line?'

'Well, yes, I do sometimes. I always feel that one shouldn't plan them ahead. For some reason, if they are spontaneous, they always seem to be much more fun. A couple of weeks ago I pushed an apricot and meringue flan into someone's face.'

'Marvellous!' breathed Kelvin.

'Shall I put the broken glasses on your bill, Sir?' asked Julian.

'Yes, do that,' said the Henry dismissively. He turned back to Kelvin. 'Why don't you all come over and join us for a drink and then have dinner with us?'

'I don't mind if I do,' Kelvin replied, dumping his half-pint tankard and deftly swiping the one remaining spirit glass off the bar before following him across to the others.

Julian looked sourly after him. 'So much for Kelvin's desire to sweep up the mess.'

The air-marshal, now that the danger of being injured by flying glass had passed, stepped cautiously through the doorway and into the room. 'You, Sir!'

Julian looked round rather wearily. 'Me, Sir?'

'Yes, you, Sir! What the Hades do you mean by allowing that sort of behaviour?'

'I'm very sorry if it upset you, Sir!'

'Upset me? Of course it upset me, and the old girl's in a terrible state out there.'

'I do apologize, Sir, and I'm extremely sorry that your wife is distressed.'

'Wife? What are you talking about, man?'

The customer was always right, of course, but Julian had to make a perceptible effort to contain himself and respond in an adequately obsequious fashion. 'I do apologize,' he said again, 'but I thought you said that your wife was in a bit of a state.'

'The dog, you fool, the dog. Bugger the wife!'

'I'd prefer not to, Sir.'

Julian received a sharp kick on the ankle from the commander and made a big effort to pull himself together. 'Once again, Sir, I am most extremely awfully sorry about the incident.'

The air-marshal snorted. 'It's quite disgraceful. This used to be a decent hotel but you seem to be cramming it with peasants and hooligans.'

The peasants were not going to lie down beneath that one. Bill stirred. 'Now look'ee here, Mister . . .'

Julian was not going to allow half-pint buyers to give any lip to his bed-buying customers. 'Shut up!' he said savagely out of the corner of his mouth. Bill looked outraged and opened his mouth again, but Julian had someone on whom he felt he could relieve his feelings: 'Shut your bloody mouth.' Bill did but the air-marshal didn't.

'How dare you talk to that man like that! You should be ashamed of yourself. You're a disgrace to your trade and if you think I am going to stay here a moment longer, you are mistaken.' The air-marshal was being extremely loud in his disapproval and he had even penetrated the miasma of booze and bonhomie round the Henrys who were passing ribald comments about the noise he was making. Julian looked down at the floor, considered the mass of splinters that were being ground into the carpet and thought briefly about the air-marshal's point before deciding that a man sometimes had to do what a man had to do, even if he had to do it to a paying customer.

'That suits me fine,' he said curtly. 'I shall make out your bill and you can be on your way.'

The air-marshal turned even redder. 'What? You're throwing me out? You horrid little poo-puncher!'

Julian may have worn rather colourful sweaters; in fact he was currently wearing a pink, chunky-knit cardigan which had a cord sewn round the neck ending in two large pom-poms dangling just below his waist, but even he was not accustomed to that type of description. The Henrys, too, thought it a little strong. There were rhubarb noises from their corner, amid which phrases like 'I say!' and 'Steady on!' were discernible. The locals just sat and marvelled, although their brains were clicking as they filed away the expression for retrieval during the long winter evenings in the pub where it could be mulled over, savoured and discussed amid the company of their peers.

If one is slightly out of the norm in one's sexual predelictions and one is prepared to come out of the closet to face the world, few of the words of man hold terrors. The concept which was embodied in the insult may have been shocking to some but, presumably, it was part of Julian's life. At any rate, he could handle himself. He rose to his feet and approached the air-marshal.

'You are not a gentleman, Sir.' The effect was devastating. It was not so much the words used as his cardigan. He had been sitting on one of the pom-poms and, when he got to his feet, it remained wedged between his legs. As he stretched to his full height in order to add dignity to his pronouncement, the cord stretched as well. The pom-pom catapulted free and struck the air-marshal on the chest. He let out a hoarse cry of horror at the sight of this circular pink object erupting from the vicinity of Julian's loins and sat heavily down on the floor. There was just time for the commander to murmur 'Oh dear' before he gave tongue again. This time it was a scream.

'What's wrong with him?' asked Bill, looking dispassionately down at the air marshal.

'He's just sat down on all the glass,' replied the commander.

'Shit!' said Julian and suddenly became the hotelier once more, kneeling down beside the stricken warrior. 'Are you all right, Sir?'

The warrior waved his arms at him. 'Get them away from me!' Julian looked puzzled.

'I think he means the pom-poms,' said Bill.

'I'm so sorry, Sir,' said Julian, gathering his pom-poms which had been dangling rudely above the air-marshal's face and stuffing them inside the cardigan. 'Are you all right?'

'Of course I'm not all right, you bloody fool. I've cut my arse to ribbons.'

'Turn over and let me have a look,' said Julian solicitously.

'If you think I'm presenting my posterior like a blasted baboon to someone like you, you're mistaken. Call a doctor, immediately.'

'I could call the doctor, but he won't come out,' said Julian. 'He never does when it's good gardening weather.'

'Call an ambulance, then.'

'It takes forty-five minutes to come.'

'This is unbelievable! I got better attention when I was shot down over Berlin.'

'There's a vet here.'

'He'll do. Tell him to hurry up before I bleed to death.'

Julian beckoned Bernard out of the crowd. 'For Christ's sake, do the best you can,' he whispered. 'If this bastard doesn't sue, there'll be a few quid in it for you.'

'And if he does sue?'

'That's the ticket, lad,' said Bill approvingly. He took a benevolent interest in the progressive loss of innocence that Bernard had undergone since his arrival in the community.

'What do you mean?' asked Julian. The air-marshal began to groan.

'If he does sue, how much will you give me?'

'A tenner?'

'A tenner a stitch.'

'But how many stitches will he need?'

'I won't know until I turn him over.' He came forward and looked down at the air-marshal who was still lying flat on the ground. 'Good evening, Sir.'

'He always is a polite lad,' said Bill approvingly.

'Would you mind turning over so that I can look at your . . . er . . . wounds?'

'I'm not a bloody Indian fakir, you fool,' replied the injured man. 'If I turn over, I'll chop my front side to bits as well.'

'Oh, yes,' said Bernard. 'Julian, can we carry this gentleman to his room where I can examine him more easily?'

Patrick came out from behind the bar and, with the help of Bill and Ivor, the air-marshal was carefully lifted up and carried out into the lobby, his backside gently dripping blood on to the carpet as they went. Julian then firmly closed the bar door in the accusing faces of the other guests.

'I reckon this will set the hotel back ten years,' he said bitterly. 'Once word gets around about what has happened, all the old goats will go and stay somewhere else.' He walked round to the other side of the bar. 'I'm going to get drunk.'

'That's what I call a damn good idea,' said the commander. 'I'll have a barley wine.'

The locals and the Henrys joined forces in response to the obvious disapproval of the other hotel guests. The Henry party was originally for a dozen but there were now eight locals too, so Julian went through to the kitchen to order extra food and more place settings in the dining room. He then temporarily abdicated his position at the helm of the hotel to Patrick. Patrick had enough sense to delay the serving of the bachelor dinner until as many of the other guests as possible had cleared from the dining room. It worked in one way, but it also gave those in the bar considerable time to fill themselves with strong drink. By the time Patrick summoned them through, the locals, including Julian, had caught up with the Henrys, and one look at them as they entered the dining room drove out the few lingering diners faster than a fire alarm.

It was a good meal. The Henrys were in full cry, subjecting waiters and waitresses to a barrage of bread rolls whenever they entered the dining room. After a few tentative lobs, Kelvin, Bill and most of the other locals were bouncing their rolls off the kitchen door and the skulls of the staff with all the aplomb of heirs to an earldom.

The staff gave almost as good as they got. Julian's young

men from the Buggery may have found the hailstorm intimidating, but the waitresses were stout-hearted country girls who were only too delighted to return the missiles launched by their Uncles Bill and Kelvin and Cousin Ivor. Julian was a little twitchy about this. His bread rolls were extremely high-class, which meant that they were as hard as bricks. It was not injury to his employees that concerned him but damage to the room. The dining room was the architectural high point of the hotel as half of it had been a Victorian conservatory. Across the centre of the room was a line of arches, beyond which both the roof and the walls were glazed, so that diners could look out over the floodlit lawn stretching down to the river.

It was nearly midnight before the meal ended. Julian was as pissed as anyone else, although he retained sufficient control to mark down in his little book stains on the carpet from spilled wine and a broken French window which one Henry was forced to kick open on his way to relieve himself on the flowerbed.

Then the glass-smashing Henry suggested a midnight swim in the river. It was thought to be an excellent idea. The entire group piled into the hotel's minibus and weaved an erratic course to the pool about half a mile up from the hotel where most of the villagers washed the dust of the day's work from themselves on hot, lazy afternoons. Those over forty did not actually swim but sat on the bank in the moonlight with Julian, who had brought along a couple of bottles of whisky to keep the party well lubricated. The summer night was full of horrid shapes and shrieks and sights unholy, the chief of which was Kelvin who got a bit over-excited and removed his teeth so that he could go round biting the pimply naked buttocks of the Henrys without becoming too intimately involved.

We returned to the hotel along the deserted lanes. Locals knew that post-midnight driving was dangerous and, if sober oneself, it was politic to park by the verge and abandon one's own car if another set of headlights came into view, gleaming on the telephone wires. Percy had made his position clear a few weeks after he had come to the village and seen the amount of drinking that went on. He was willing to chase drunks if that was what the public wanted, but they would have to live with the consequence that most of them would be deprived of their licences within a few months. His advice to the minority who were sober after closing time was that they keep off the road. The van came to a juddering halt in front of the hotel and its passengers disembarked to stand around trying to remember whether they were supposed to be staying at the hotel or if they had homes to go to. There was a shriek from Julian.

'Look at my bloody lawn!'

We looked at his bloody lawn.

'What about it?' asked Kelvin, gazing rather blearily across it. The floodlights were still on, no doubt ticking up like a taxi meter inside Julian's little book.

'There's a bloody great furrow across it! No there isn't. Look! There are two bloody great furrows across it.'

'Oh yes, so there are. I wonder how that happened?' mused the commander.

Julian was virtually frothing at the mouth. The froth might have been worth collecting and bottling to be sold as blanched advocaat, for it must have been seventy per cent proof. 'It's obvious, isn't it? Some drunken bastard has driven across it. It's ruined.' He turned to his guests. 'I bet it was one of you lot.'

The Henrys clutched each other for support and formed a defensive circle like a wagon train under Indian attack in face of Julian's venom. 'It was all right when I went out for a piss before we went swimming,' said the pissing Henry. 'I remember thinking what a superb croquet lawn it would make.'

'That's quite true,' said Kelvin, nodding owlishly.

'You would have been too drunk to notice,' snapped Julian.

'I don't mean the furrows. I mean the croquet lawn.'

'Oh, I see.'

'It must have been done by someone when we were out,' said a Henry.

'Of course!' cried Julian. 'Let's find out who's come back late.'

'Or went out late,' added the Henry. There was one member of staff still up – one of the younger cooks, who was sitting disconsolately in the hall. His blue eyes lit up as he saw Julian burst through the door.

'Julian! I thought you were never coming back,' he said. 'I thought you must have been drowned.'

'Don't be silly, Simon.'

'I'm not being silly. You said we'd have some time together this evening. And look what's happened. It's two o'clock in the morning. You just don't care any more.'

Everyone else started to make tactfully loud conversation just outside the front door while Julian sorted out his domestic arrangements. About five minutes later he came out again. 'I can't understand it. According to Simon, nobody has been in or out since we left.'

'That's not so difficult to understand,' said the commander. 'I've been thinking about it and it's obvious, isn't it? It must have been the minibus we were in that messed up the lawn. We were all so drunk that nobody noticed.'

'That's it!' said Julian in a state of great excitement. 'It was us. Who was driving?'

'Well, I was on the way there—' began the commander.

'You bastard!' exclaimed Julian. 'I might have known it would be you.'

'But I can't have gone over the lawn because the van was parked halfway down the drive and the tyre tracks come right up here. It must have been done on the retun journey just now.'

'Oh, I see. Well, who drove on the way back?' asked Julian.

'I don't remember,' said the commander.

The guests and the locals were beginning to mill around in the same disjointed, headless-chicken fashion which can be observed in the few Glaswegian pedestrians who are abroad on 1 January. Julian called them to order. Rage had burned up most of the alcohol in his bloodstream. 'Who was driving the minibus on the way back? Kelvin?'

'It wasn't me,' replied Kelvin hurriedly. 'I can remember sitting in the back, trying to get my teeth back in.'

'And I was lying on the floor,' said a Henry.

'And it wasn't me, because I was sitting in the passenger seat at the front,' said Ivor.

Julian spun on his heel towards him. 'Aha! If you were sitting in the passenger seat, you must have seen who was driving. Who was it?' Ivor shut his eyes in an effort to remember and Bill put out a supporting hand as he moved dangerously out of the perpendicular. He opened them again. 'I can't recall.'

'Of course you bloody can. You're just not trying,' said Julian in frustration. 'Think, man. Did you talk to him?'

Ivor shut his eyes again. 'I don't think I talked to him. Hang on a minute. Of course! He was singing!'

'Singing! What?' demanded Julian.

Ivor thought again and his face crumpled in disappointment. 'I don't know. I knew the tune, but I couldn't understand the words. They were foreign. It was all about psychologists. In German. Freud and Jung and something. It was that tune that the children always play on their recorders at the carol service.'

'Psychologists? Freud?' Julian looked baffled for a few seconds as he thought. Then his face cleared. 'Of course! *Freude, schöner Gotterfunken,*' he sang. 'Beethoven's Ninth!'

'That's it!' said Ivor.

'Right! Now we're getting somewhere. Who knows Beethoven's Ninth?' He received blank looks from everyone. 'Come on: *Freude, schöner Gotterfunken, Tochter aus Elysium*! Someone must know it.'

Kelvin broke the ensuing silence by clearing his throat.

'Yes, Kelvin?' said Julian.

'It occurs to me,' said Kelvin, 'that you are probably the only person who knows it.'

'Well, yes, I do know it. But so what?'

'Then it stands to reason that you were sitting beside Ivor and that it must have been you that was driving and it was you that ran over the lawn.'

'Oh, come off it,' said Julian, a bit uncertainly. 'I would have remembered.'

'And there's another thing,' continued Kelvin implacably, 'you've been holding the van's ignition keys in your hand for the last half-hour.'

It was game, set and match to Kelvin and everyone went to bed.

Julian reckoned later that, in spite of hitting the Henrys for well over £1000, he lost on the weekend. It was the air-marshal's fault. He did not sue, but probably cost Julian more through lost bookings than he would have succeeded in winning in damages. Julian even had to write off the Henrys' breakfast bill.

The morning after the night before, Julian had laid on the most expensive breakfast he could devise. It was to be his last opportunity of wresting any money from their capacious wallets. Kelvin and Ivor had failed to make it home the night before and they, as pale and delicate as the Henrys, had been rousted out of their temporary accommodation in the resident's lounge by the staff. There was a large circular table laid out in the glassed portion of the dining room on which Julian had laid out the whole works from kedgeree through champagne and kippers, kidneys, figs, porridge and all items in the hotel's deep freeze that may not have had the legs to stagger on for very much longer. There was a whole platter of tiny trout. The fact that those for whom it was intended were incapable of doing more than trickle into the room to sip delicately at glasses of grapefruit juice, nurse their blinding hangovers and dread the responsibilities, the noise and the need for polite conversation that lay before them as ushers at the wedding, was immaterial to him in his search for profit. They came in, one by one, to sit in silence trying to ignore the thunder of the bluebottles, trapped under the glass of the dining-room roof.

The air-marshal had been nursing his injuries in his bedroom since his accident the night before. Bernard had sprayed his bottom with purple veterinary Terramycin from an aerosol can, bandaged it and advised him to stay in bed for a day or two to give it a chance to heal. To keep him away from the telephone and his solicitor, Julian had sent a couple of bottles of gin up to his bedroom and the air-marshal had spent a sleepless night finishing them to ensure that he could demand some more in the morning.

What goes in must come out, and the air-marshal no longer had the capacity of bladder that he had enjoyed in his youth. Because of this, he had developed the custom of carrying his own chamber pot with him wherever he went. This saved him from the need to tramp the corridors of strange houses and hotels in search of a bathroom during the still watches of the night. His habit was to empty the utensil the following morning.

So far, so good. But the air-marshal had cut his bum and had drunk the best part of two bottles of gin, so he did not feel like walking all the way to the bathroom when it came to pass that his pot was due to be emptied. Circumstances were building up with the remorseless precision of a Shakespearean tragedy.

In the dining room, life was beginning to stir. The room had filled up with the other guests, silent save for the clicking of false teeth as they chomped their way through bacon and eggs and the rustle as they turned the pages of *The Times* and the *Daily Telegraph*. Even the Henrys were beginning to realize that it was possible to function, provided that they did not move their heads too quickly, and started to pick over the trout and nibble tentatively at the kidneys. It was Kelvin who provided the catalyst for their revival. He was not sure whether he would be asked to pay for his breakfast or if Julian would slap it all on the Henrys' bill. He did know, however, that he would not be asked for more than his tithe. No hangover could prevent him from eating, given his awareness that the food might be free, or at least reduced in cost the more he ate. The sight of him sturdily ploughing through as many different dishes as possible, secure in the knowledge that Prudence was doing the morning agricultural chores, inspired the others to action. Conversation even broke out.

'What time are you on duty?' asked Ivor.

'I think we're all meant to be meeting somewhere for lunch, but I'm not sure where,' replied the Henry to whom this remark was addressed. 'Are you coming?'

'He is, but I'm not,' replied Kelvin. 'They didn't invite me.'

'Oh, what a shame!' said the Henry. He really did seem rather sorry, which showed how little he knew Kelvin.

'A wedding like that is not for the likes of me,' said Kelvin, helping himself to a kipper and putting a poached egg on top of it. There was a silver bowl full of roses in the centre of the table and Kelvin looked as if he might start on that, once he'd cleared the rest of the table. The other Henrys were beginning to realize the danger and were taking kedgeree and bacon while there was still some left.

'Oh, you really must come. It'll be such fun and I'm sure nobody will mind. Nobody would notice you in the crush at the reception, anyway.'

Kelvin seemed mildly interested in the idea so Ivor

hurriedly broke in. 'I think Kelvin would be noticed. It would be awfully rude to go without an invitation, and anyway Kelvin hasn't got any clothes.'

'I've got the suit that I wore to the Loosemire wedding last year,' said Kelvin indignantly.

'You need a morning coat,' said Ivor. 'A tail coat.'

'What does a tail coat look like?' asked Kelvin.

Most of the Henrys had already put on their striped trousers. One had on his waistcoat and jacket too and he put down his coffee cup and stood up to rotate for Kelvin's benefit.

The air-marshal was a traditionalist. He did not like waste and the precious nitrogen in his pot was far better spread on the flowerbed beneath his window, he felt, than poured away down the sewers. He did not believe in investing in a modern chamber pot, even if such things existed; he preferred a pretty antique one with flowers all over it. A Victorian pot might inculcate the Victorian virtues that made the Empire. But the pot was in much the same condition as the Empire and the air-marshal had never really bothered to look out of his window to admire the view. Up in his room, the air-marshal had crawled over to the window and hung out his pot. He rotated it so that its contents would void themselves into the flowerbed beneath. As his wrist started to turn, incalculable forces were unleashed upon the join between the handle and the main body of the utensil and they parted. It was not the fault of the century-dead potter, but of the quality of the glue that the air-marshal had used a couple of years previously to join the two together.

The defenestration of the pot as well as the contents was accidental, but the air-marshal's lack of reconnaissance beforehand was criminally negligent. The combination of booze and bottom must have clouded his judgement. The flowerbed was not there at all. Instead, the pot met the glass roof of the dining room and plunged through in a blizzard of splinters, losing scarcely any of its momentum. It retained its physical integrity until it struck the silver rose bowl in the midst of the pre-nuptial breakfast, whereupon it exploded. The roses leapt out of the bowl to escape, falling amid the kippers and kidneys, but they were overwhelmed by a shower of flowery fragments of pottery and a great, golden sunburst of processed gin which spread outward, dissipating in quantity and in speed of progress to break feebly against the extremities of the room. Barely a breakfaster escaped from at least part of the fall-out, while the wedding guests endured its full force.

The gerontocrats reacted first. With hoots and bellows of rage and dismay, they rose from their tables and vacated the dining room. Reaction was slower from the wedding party. The Henry who had been standing up had had his back to the table at the moment of impact and was not fully aware of the nature of the disaster. He turned and sat down as the first of the Henrys picked up his napkin, delicately re-folded it inside out and began to mop his face.

Kelvin expressed the mood of the moment. With urine

dripping from his chin, he surveyed the devastated table. 'Thank God there was a cover on the kedgeree. That'll keep us going until they bring some more food.'

Kelvin made the wedding. Julian unearthed a trunk of ancient tail coats and trousers in the attic of the hotel which had been part of the uniform of the hotel staff fifty years earlier and these were handed out to the wedding guests whose own garments had blotted up most of the explosion. There was one set that fitted Kelvin and he was smuggled into the church by the ushers. He even achieved fame. Three months later the festivities featured in the society section of one of the glossies. There was a picture of a group of guests, taken after the service beneath the Virginia-creeper-clad clock tower of the church as the bells rang out in celebration. Princess Peter Grimescu and the Hon. Michael Berkeley-Howard were in animated conversation with each other, while a third figure leered at the photographer over the princess's shoulder. Somebody had tried to touch up his teeth and airbrush out some of his spiky grey hair, but it was not necessary to read the caption to identify him. Mr Kelvin Morchard went out and bought eighty copies of the magazine.